Elizabeth Latham had a worldwide career in theatre and opera before she discovered the letters that inspired this book. She has been a stage manager at Stratford-on-Avon Shakespeare Theatre, at the Glyndebourne Opera House, the technical director for many of the Edinburgh Festivals and also the first manager for the 'Philharmonia Hungarica' orchestra, founded in Vienna after the Hungarian revolution, and she was the very first woman to be appointed stage director at the Royal Opera House, Covent Garden. *Silences of the Heart* is her first novel.

Elizabeth Latham

SILENCES
OF
THE HEART

First published in this edition in 1997
by HEADLINE BOOK PUBLISHING

A REVIEW paperback

10 9 8 7 6 5 4 3 2

ISBN 0 7472 5640 3

Printed and bound in Great Britain by
Clays Ltd, St Ives plc

HEADLINE BOOK PUBLISHING
A division of Hodder Headline PLC
338 Euston Road
London NW1 3BH

FOR MY FAMILY

and especially in memory of those in this story.
It is on their letters and diaries that I have based this tale.

CONTENTS

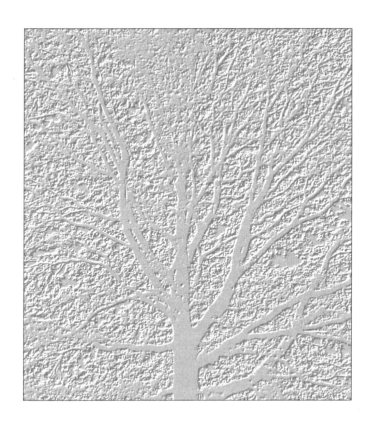

PART ONE

CLAUDIA'S STORY
– From Her Diary

INTRODUCTION

I N THE FAMILY around whom this tale is written, three generations emigrated in silence, not in search of adventure or another climate, but to escape – for various reasons. The third generation is Claudia Carfax, now a well-known portrait painter. She was born in 1906 in the then sparsely populated Cowichan Valley on Vancouver Island. In 1927, when she was 21, she left by train and steamer for Europe, to study painting in London and Florence. Hers was the classic escape of youth who have limited opportunities in the lands of their birth.

Now, 45 years later, she is living in Vienna, in a large studio apartment covering the entire attic floor of a tall building on the north bank of the Danube, where the river curves away so that one can see not only the commercial barges and the passenger steamers but also far over to the sloping vineyards and to the church spire in the wooded hills above. She has lived there for 18 of her 66 years and has never grown tired of the view.

It is eight o'clock in the morning but she has been up since the early hours. The studio floor is covered in crates of various sizes into which she is packing the last of her canvases – 35 works in all. They will shortly be shown at a spring exhibition, which posters in the city are advertising as: "The Latest Works of Claudia Carfax – The Mask of Vienna".

There is a triple ring at the door-bell. She runs to open

the door, expecting to see the men from the art gallery's transport firm.

But there is only a young boy, holding out a cable.

```
MOTHER FAILING STOP ASKING FOR YOU STOP
WILL MEET PLANE AT VICTORIA STOP CABLE
ARRIVAL TIME STOP HURRY STOP
JOHN
```

And so Claudia starts on the long journey back into her past.

SATURDAY, MAY 6TH

(*In the plane from Vienna*)

I have decided to put down my thoughts in this notebook during the long flight. There will be plenty of time for thinking. First, I must never forget how kind and understanding Director Braunsteg has been; of course, he knows that these latest portraits are some of my best work. It has taken a lifetime, but now I am "a collector's item". How odd that is! For, to me, I am still that same raw Canadian girl who dared to hire the Church Hall in Duncan, all those years ago, for her first one-woman show.

Now Aunt Faith is calling me home. It will be a fearfully sad return.

Director Braunsteg said that he will explain away my absence from the *vernissage* to the press with the moving story of the artist suddenly having to return to her native bush under tragic circumstances. It will at least be a new publicity story.

NOON

It was a smooth flight over the Alps to London Airport and now I am surrounded by the accents, food and magazines of Air Canada. I am being taken care of by a familiar nanny.

The lunch was excellent. Aunt Faith always said that I was probably the only person in the world who would ask for a second helping of the hangman's dinner. Two glasses of Bordeaux have made me sleepy. I sit alone, as early May is an out-of-season time and the plane is only half full . . . I must have slept a long while for we are being asked to fasten our seat-belts for the landing at Vancouver Airport and the plane is late.

AT HOME — AT MIDNIGHT

I had to make a dash through the airport to catch the connecting plane to the island and there, at the Pat Bay airport, stood dear John. It was only 30 hours since I had received his cable in Vienna but over nine years since we had last seen each other at his wife's funeral. Nine years since I last saw the island and my home.

During the familiar drive up and over the Malahat Range, (surely one of the world's most beautiful views?), John explained how his mother had suddenly become dangerously frail after having a heart attack, two days ago. Her theme-song for over 20 years has always been, "I'm sticking at 70. It's a grand age to be!" But now she is 93 and not a day younger.

Nothing here has changed, simply nothing. Even John's old car seems to be the same. And the road too. The black-top ends abruptly, just where it always ended, and then the car's wheels throw up the same gritty stones and dust as we turn into our lane. The ruts are the same, as we lurch from side to side, the brambles scratching the windows of the car, the firs overhead as straight and as black as ever.

Suddenly all that I have worked for and achieved in a lifetime in Europe, and all my personal problems, are completely uninteresting and totally unimportant. Everything falls into place. I am just their Claudia, come home to help, and the only urgency is to get there in time to see Aunt alive.

All the lights were on in the house, to welcome me, Aunt Faith's prodigal child, back home again.

TUESDAY, MAY 9TH

Aunt Faith is still very much alive, and absolutely thrilled that I have come.

"Darling love, how simply wonderful to see you again! How much I have longed for you to be here and you are just in time for the dogwoods!"

These are the first simple and genuinely loving words that I have heard for months and certainly the most intelligent evaluation of my visit, both for her and for me. The blooming of the dogwoods was always our symbol of hope, year after year, and the proof of yet another hard winter safely weathered.

How Uncle Gerald and Aunt Faith struggled with the farm, to make it pay against the freakishness of the island's weather, each year seeming to bring the deepest floods or the driest summer since God knows when, and John and I helped them, just as soon as we were strong enough to carry a pail of water or tall enough to use a rake. Much later, my personal struggle was to prove to them that I had it in me to be an artist, a real professional one, with an exhibition in some big town to clinch it.

I have never stopped drawing, ever since I could first hold a small piece of chalk in my fist and scribble on my slate – anything, everything. I always loved faces best but no one had the time, then, to sit for me, except on Saturday evenings after bath-time. Sundays have always been kept by Aunt as the Day of Rest, only excepting the unavoidable demands from the livestock. Otherwise, it was off to church, or reading, writing letters home to family and friends in the Old Country and making music after supper. Aunt Faith has always been "Aunt" to me even after she and Uncle Gerald adopted me; she never wanted my memories of my mother to fade, or to usurp her in any way. Now Aunt is bedridden but so cheerfu. Her nightgown smells of garden lavender from the sachets in her cupboards and the sheets and blankets are fresh from being dried in the wind and sun. No dry-cleaning chemicals nor scummy laundry odours for her! She is not a scrap deaf, her hair is still tawny-grey and her misty eyes twinkle, seeing everything only too clearly, and without spectacles. Her teeth are a bit sparse and the old hands are arthritically clawed inwards. Her face is as lined as an admiralty chart, fascinating to draw.

We have spent three whole days together, just we two, over endless pots of tea, filling in all the details of my years of rather sketchy correspondence. She has always been a great sender-on of interesting news-clippings out of the local rag and from the *Colonist*. She has kept me in touch with the island. In return, I have kept her informed of my successes. Glowing reviews or articles about my work were, frankly, only of interest to me in so far as they made her and Uncle Gerald happy and proud of me. So I sent her the cuttings and translated the best bits out of the continental papers. The negative ones I held back to chew over alone, painfully, and then to throw away.

I remember Benjamin Britten once telling me that he never read any of his critics and, in fact, only took the local Suffolk paper. "The daily weather report is what interests me most," he said, "and if there is a revolution or the Queen dies, the news will eventually reach the headlines, even in Aldeburgh."

How desperately tired I am. It is not only jet-lag but weeks of anxiety-ridden nights. Could I complete everything in time? Would this important show succeed? How grateful I was for that first night here at home. In my old room off the living-room, in the same mahogany bed with the chintz flounces, I slept for ten hours and woke the next morning with a child's hot cheeks and a roaring appetite for a substantial Canadian breakfast.

Friday, May 12th

Aunt Faith, always practical and never one for wasting time, said to me on the third day, "Now that you are here, darling love, I am going to make use of you. I may be called to the Lord at any minute and I am certainly not going to survive another heart attack. Actually I'm only still here because, after Dr McKenzie pulled me through and John told me that he had cabled for you to come, I was most certainly not going to miss you. We have talked everything over and we both want you to help us by clearing out and tidying up all the rooms, one by one. Since the girls left home to get married and since dear Janet died, John has all he can manage to keep the farm and the property going. I'm no chicken but he's not getting any younger either and the loss of Janet has aged him a lot. I'm sure you've noticed this, although he's lucky to have kept his thick curly hair and to have inherited my eyesight. I've hoarded all my life and let things slip badly, I admit it, but I've never wanted Ethel to sort out drawers and cupboards and personal things. She's grand for the cooking and general cleaning and I am so grateful to have had her all these years – such a good, honest soul. But family is family, so be a dear and start on the dining-room tomorrow."

And so I have started on the strict understanding that I throw away only what she calls "my rat-packer hoardings". Anything very personal or doubtful, I am collecting in shoe-boxes – she has simply dozens of these – and then I put them on a table pulled up to her bed, where she can go through them herself, slowly, in her own time, box by box.

Of course, even on the first day, she called me a thouand times, to share in the contents of over 70 years of correspondence, picking out the plums with chuckles and hoots of laughter and illuminating comments. I thought she might die of laughing before she had finished even one box.

So I started to cheat, concealing those boxes filled only with old envelopes, Christmas, Easter and birthday cards, church magazines, and catalogues from sales, some from way back in the 1930s and '40s. I crept out with them hidden under my large apron and made a bonfire down at the far end of the yard, well out of sight and smell of her window, feeling terribly guilty, but knowing we'd never get anywhere otherwise.

It is all such fun, such enormous fun, this do-you-remember? game, this revival of my own rose-coloured childhood memories and adolescent panics, and of three generations of Aunt's family born, married and dead. It gives one such a sense of proportion again, like standing back from the easel, setting a distance between oneself and life.

The farm, "Frome", has not altered one bit. The garden has matured, of course, and now a Chinaman, Mr Wei, is putting his whole heart into it. The Chinese are such fine gardeners! I suppose we learned the art of gardening from them, perhaps through the Babylonians.

Now it is Friday evening. All Wednesday, Thursday and today I have ploughed my way through the dining-room chaos, accompanied by shouts of "Whatever are you up to now? You've been completely silent for over an hour. I'm sure you are up to no good in there!" So I go in to reassure her and she reads me yet another forgotten secret out of an old letter, a friend's *mésalliance* way back in 1923. Then I return to the drawers and the shelves, sorting and reading, sifting and rejecting. A now-tired little voice calls to me. "I would so like a cup of very sweet tea and some digestive biscuits." So I leave everything piled on the dining-room table, to sort things out after our tea break.

In this dining-room, seated around the table, Aunt Faith taught us – John and me. I remember so well that when I was stuck over some tricky question, I would concentrate by fixing my gaze on the row of poplars separating the drive from the first meadow, where the horses grazed. Uncle and Aunt planted the young trees on their wedding-day, as a future wind-break. Now the trees must be at least 90 feet tall and have stood through over 60 years of the island's storms.

All the furniture in the dining-room has become "antique" and the dealers are always pressing Aunt to sell. They all know what she has, since that day when she foolishly asked one to call in and value a clock. "Absurd!" she says. "We would now be eating all our meals off the floor. He wanted the dining-room table, the eight rush-seated chairs with the spindle backs, the oak side-board and the glass-fronted china cabinet, not to mention all the carpets and rugs."

There is no china in the cabinet; it is all kept in the kitchen instead, strong, everyday, willow-patterned. We have had only that as long as I can remember. Instead, the cabinet was crammed with receipted bills, check-stubs, newspaper-cuttings, calendars, one with "Fond loving thoughts from all the family in Frome, Xmas 1921". A life-time reduced to a pile of jammed shoe-boxes and hillocks of paper, now blackening into ashes in the yard.

I feel simply awful about this, this anticipation of death, for that is what it is. I keep running to her room to make sure that she is still alive, bless her!

Today was my *vernissage* and it will be over by now — nine hours' difference in time between here and Vienna. It simply does not matter a hoot to me. The only important thing is to get the dining-room finished by tomorrow evening, so that Sunday can be kept as it always has been at "Frome", as the Lord's Day.

At about four o'clock, I glanced in at Aunt, but she was still deep in her afternoon sleep, puffing away contentedly, an old letter in one hand.

Now, suddenly, I am reminded of my Hungarian friend, Ilona Banat: such a beautiful woman, years ago in London. She was married to a very wealthy South American diplomat, charming her husband as well as her lovers and boasting, so delightfully and wittily, of her successful "salon" and of her scalp-hunting. She had her finger in every pie. I first saw her when she swept in in her winter furs to one of our student shows. Heaven only knows why she took me up. I was only a young nobody, a Canadian raw-bone, studying art on a scholarship at the Slade School. With great perspicacity, she kindly invited me, each Tuesday, to an enormous, life-saving lunch and then gave me money, tactfully in an envelope, for the afternoons I spent cataloguing her husband's library in their gorgeous home in Onslow Square.

We've always kept in touch and now she lives in Vienna, a poor widow, sick and alone, the riches all spent and the lovers gone – the last one with the remains of her jewellery. I visited her just before coming here. She said that she now had no one in her life who cared whether she ever got into or out of a bed again. I was cold with sadness for her. "But it matters to you," I said, simply because I had somehow to bridge the awkward silence. "No, my dear, nothing matters to me if I am not the centre of someone's life," she replied. What depths of nihilism! Her life is now slithering away at a snail's pace, in a dusty, under-heated room in an unfashionable district in Vienna. Indeed, how can she bear it? Is old Ilona at this moment thinking of me, after yet another of her endless lonely nights? Will that sort of end be my fate, too?

As I stood in the bedroom doorway, looking at Aunt lying in her sun-filled room, in the house that Uncle Gerald built for her, furnished with a lifetime of wonderful memories and filled with her humour and warmth, courage and determination, John came in from the farm for a cup of tea.

He crept up behind me. "This is how a life should end," he whispered, and went very quietly into the kitchen to put the kettle on the fire.

CLAUDIA'S STORY

That was a really good day's work to look back on and grand to feel all those aching muscles, now eased slightly looser after tonight's hot mustard bath. My hair is shampooed, too. It was filthy.

Ethel had told me that one can hire a carpet-shampooing apparatus from the local drugstore, so John drove me down to the town, first thing after breakfast. "It's cheaper to hire at the special weekend rate," said Ethel, "and why throw good money down the drain?" As she controls the housekeeping purse and accounts to Aunt for every cent, I followed instructions.

Ethel helped me to roll the heavy carpets from both the dining-room and the living-room out onto the verandah, where I laid them out flat and shampooed them, and then we hung them over the orchard fence to dry. The sun was blazing hot and the air so dehydrated that they dried out quite quickly. The old William Morris curtains I had washed cold, on Friday evening in the bath, fearing that they would fall apart, but they have survived and I pegged them out on the line in the yard to dry overnight, not daring to risk exposing them to the boiling sun. Their colours are as fresh and almost as strong as ever. Nothing can beat a first-class vintage Irish linen. What pride one has over successful domestic chores!

The cedar-wood floor, which Aunt reminded me that Uncle William, my darling uncle, had laid single-handed, is still lovely. The naturally oily wood is now dark and glowing from 60 years of Aunt's polishing, with some years of mine, and crowned by years of what Ethel calls "me elbow grease". Ethel has spent most of her life in Canada but has never lost her Cockney accent. So, while Ethel was on her knees polishing, I ironed all the curtains and then cleaned the pictures, mostly photos of the Frome crowd, three generations of them, playing tennis in ankle-length dresses, their hair in *bandeaux*; or cycling over the Somersetshire hills in bloomers and tight-waisted blouses, the men with Harrow boaters; first-borns, proudly held up, squinting into the sun, including John; and then that photo of my mother, radiant as she stands arm-in-arm with Uncle William, both of them so handsome and elegant in tailored winter coats and Mother so dashing in a little bearskin fur cap with a matching muff.

This dining-room is a charming room, opening on to the verandah on the sunny side of the house. How well planned the whole home is! Uncle Carlo designed it all, Aunt once told me, and built it with help from our neighbour, old Mac, and from Uncle William, and of course, from Uncle Gerald.

How Aunt loves to go back to the good old days, particularly to talk about my mother, her "lovely Antonia"! Those two young women built up a unique friendship and Aunt must have loved my mother greatly to have adopted me at Mother's death, when my father did not know what to do with me. I was then just three, a late child. My father was always away, working on the road which is now the highway from Victoria to Port Hardy.

Aunt wants very much to see the results of my efforts and is simply furious that Dr McKenzie will not let her up until the end of next week. As it is, with all the excitement of going through her old letters, she was as tired as if she had done the whole week's cleaning herself, and she fell deeply into her night's sleep at around eight p.m., after enjoying a glass of hot milk with her favourite clover honey.

The evening was so warm that J and I sat for ages after supper, out on the verandah, quietly talking. At least J talked and I listened. He needed that. He is such a lonely man and so grateful for what I am doing in the home to help them.

2:30 A.M.

I can manage the days very successfully. It is the nights that get me down. In the daytime, I am their Claudia. I think, feel and act spontaneously and impulsively like a young girl. There is no time for introversion, for wallowing in sick memories, for analytical acrobatics.

For a year or two, as far as my private life in Vienna is concerned, I have gradually become entangled in non-essentials, seeing life through other people's eyes, accepting alien values. I fitted in, kept my mouth shut, stayed out of the way — blinkered like an old nag in harness. No one here would have recognized me. Yet over the past couple of years, I've been painting better than ever, almost as if my inability to see myself gave me piercing X-ray eyes to analyse the features and the characters of other people. I know that I am a good artist and an experienced craftswoman and no one, no one, can ever take that away from me.

Where did things start to go wrong? Was I always, deep down, so unsure of myself because I started off my young adult life travelling steerage to England on a one-way ticket? Actually an emigrant, always made to feel an inferior colonial outsider?

It has just struck me that I have flown out here now on a one-way ticket. Why didn't I take a return?

SUNDAY, MAY 14TH
(*Mother's Day*)

This was a wonderful day! We started off by having a late breakfast in Aunt's bedroom. Not our meagre, take-it-or-leave-it continental breakfast but grapefruit, bacon and fried eggs, fried tomatoes with potato pancakes, homemade bread and two different homemade jams, Royal Sovereign strawberry and raspberry, apple jelly and our own honey and lashings of Earl Grey tea. Aunt ate as if she had a busy day on the farm ahead of her.

It was a glorious day; the hummingbirds darted in and out of the lilac bush in front of her open window, and then we read her the epistle and gospel for the day before setting off to church.

I had forgotten that it takes nearly an hour on foot to get there and had insisted on walking, for old times' sake. Of course we arrived late and fearfully hot but we only missed the first hymn and, as the doors had been latched back to let in any puff of breeze, we slipped in at the south side and sat in our old places, right by the open door. From there, I could see Mother's grave, under the old oak, now so freshly green and shady. Trees — Pasternak came into my mind and how he once said that he could never leave Russia because he could not bear to live away from the Russian birch woods. That is a haunting recollection and I wished that I could have shared that with Mother. She would have understood him.

I am now so short-sighted that, without my glasses, I deliberately transform life around me into a pleasant haze, but I heard folk whispering, "There's Claudia!" and John nudged me in the ribs, "The Prodigal Daughter's return." I am so happy that I start to blush, which is ridiculous at my age.

The hymns are always pitched far too high for any congregation but they were all my old favourites and I boomed happily away in a mock baritone. The preacher was a visitor from the mainland. No country man. A sermon on duty and service to others. I shut out the ponderous voice and avoided the well-fed face.

I concentrated on Mother's grave beneath a simple Celtic cross of dark local stone, under the shade of the old oak which will outlive us all. She lies alone. It is strange but I have never felt the least desire to visit my father's grave. He is buried somewhere up near Mount Norquay, in the Rockies, where he and his second wife were killed in a motoring accident. I never knew her, never wanted to meet her. Father meant nothing to me. My brother? I've not seen him since he left school and went off to Vancouver. In 1911 or 1912? He will be an old man, now – maybe dead?

After church, there was coffee and biscuits in the Church Hall and J reminded me that we must go over; it was expected of us. For some folk, this is their only social contact of the week. The distances out here are so enormous, shortened today by the car, of course, but to little real advantage. I think that motorization has cut people off even more from each other. Each racing along in his own metal and glass box, the radio blaring, instead of jogging along in the buggy as we used to do, giving a lift to a friend or two on the way, chatting together to the even rhythms of the horse's hooves.

For me, as a child, an outing began when I was sent to fetch the horse in from the meadow, to get the harness from the stable and then the cushions and empty shopping-baskets from the house. Travelling into town with Uncle Gerald, Aunt Faith and John, bumping along our lane, dodging under the lower branches, weighed down in the full-leaved summer, waving to friends, missing a hunting cat, thinking only of Joe Paynes' Bakery and of chocolate meringues with whipped cream and of how to lay out my Saturday's pocket money. Liquorice Bootlaces, Sherbert Dips, mixed Jujubes or Caramel Toffee? The tremendously important problems of childhood days and the excitement of simply going down to the town and seeing all those people, our folk and the Indians and Hindus and Chinese. Surely at least 50 people on Main Street? And sometimes even having the luck to be near the station when the train pulled in and goods and mail were unloaded and strangers got off — even folk from Europe.

I got a great welcome in the Church Hall and felt quite overwhelmed and very happy that so many still remember me. "Does this mean that you are coming back to live?" A dozen times I heard this question and my answer, "Well, for the moment I'm only here to help my aunt and my cousin John."

Here I go again, living my life as part of someone else's pattern, a tenuous shadow in a corner of another person's picture. But do I want to return to be a part of Aunt's land-scape, to live in her shadow? Being home again, I realize that absolutely nothing has altered for her. When she decided to marry, she founded a home to be the centre of her life, from where all movement and thought flowed. Her one gamble was to marry the lonely, middle-aged Uncle Gerald, and what a marvellous marriage they made of it!

After lunch, I read the latest church magazine to Aunt until she fell asleep. It was so hot that I hung the hammock out between the two pear trees, filled it with cushions and dozed the afternoon away. I offered to help with the stock, but J has his routine and also young Jim to help, and Ethel looks after the poultry, bees and pigs. I have brought with me my fear of being in the way.

This evening, after supper, we pulled Aunt's bed into the doorway of her room, placed the old blue-and-white Chinese screen protectively around her and propped the living-room door wide open so that she could see the piano. It is the same upright which Mother brought out with her by boat in 1890. The gold lettering above the keyboard, "Grotrian-Steinweg, Braunschweig. Smith of Liverpool", is scratched and dulled and one of the brass candle-holders has broken off and never been replaced. Uncle bought the piano from my father. He knew what it would mean to Aunt to have Antonia's piano.

I can remember the day when the piano was moved over to "Frome". It was the day of the move from my parents' home, "The Fens", after Father had sold it. The transportation of the piano was a real drama, for the solid iron frame took the strength of four tough young men to shift it up onto the cart, which then promptly stuck, hopelessly, in the first rut. Someone had to run to McRae's home to ask him for the loan of his pair of oxen to help with the hauling.

Then I was sat up in the cart, on the piano stool, with baskets full of music around my legs.

"Can it be a request concert?" Aunt called out from her bed. "I would like some gentle Mendelssohn first, the 9th Lied on page 27, then the 14th on page 42 and the 21st on page 68." (She knows them all by heart and the Koechel numbers for Mozart's works. A fabulous memory, even for something only seen once.) "Then Sinding's 'Rustle of Spring' – you always played that so prettily – and then some good strong Beethoven to round off with. The Rondo opus 129 would be good."

So I sorted out the music and then played for her, with unpractised, stiff fingers, but not as badly as I had feared, major and minor and back to major, the music long absorbed deep into my mind and into my fingers, long before stereo sound through loud-speakers.

Suddenly I realized that Mother had nearly always played or sung music which was written in a minor key. One day, sitting beside her on the music-stool, with my right arm tightly around her waist and my right thumb hooked into the waistband of her skirt, I suddenly could bear it no longer and tore her hands savagely from the keyboard, cutting off the deep melancholies of Grieg, the endless dark of the Norwegian winters, the icy winds blasting down from the mountains into the black fjords.

She turned to me, startled, her huge brown eyes glazed over with tears, and I knew that she had been a thousand miles away, on what she always called "my travels, my travels of the mind".

What did Mother see as she played? Did she have visions of England, of her old home, of her parents and friends? Where was she travelling? I shall never know, because I was then far too young to ask the questions and certainly not old enough to understand the answers.

The house was so quiet after the last chord of the Beethoven that I thought I had bored John into slipping out of the room and Aunt into sleeping but, turning round on the music-stool, I saw John smiling and relaxed in the grandfather chair, his head resting back on a wing, his blue eyes full of happiness.

Aunt was wide awake. "Bless you, dear child for that

music. You have given me the most lovely present imaginable for Mother's Day – you have revived all my old and fading memories." It was a wonderful day – for all of us.

MONDAY, MAY 15TH

"Another blue Monday," snorted Ethel, as she stumped out of the house with the loaded washing-basket balanced on her stomach. Not as blue as they used to be, I thought, now that the wash-house is wired up to the generator and fitted out with a washing-machine, a tumbler and an ironing roller, and now that soap powders come ready mixed out of packets. No more cutting of thin slivers of yellow Sunlight soap into the washtub. No boiler to be kept going all day, despite sudden down-draughts and unfriendly wood, no possibility of bungling with the blue-bag, resulting in a shameful clothes-line, hung with rows of sheets and underwear blotched with too much blue dye.

The district nurse came today to bed-bathe Aunt and we lifted her into the rocking-chair by the window, from where she could see much more of the garden and of her birds at their feeding-table, whilst I changed the bed-linen. Now she is lying back again in bed, in a field of fresh cotton poppies and cornflowers and wheatears. I spread an old tablecloth across her lap and brought her some more shoe-boxes.

"How lucky that you were born with dirt under your nails and know how to get down to a job," commented Aunt, tartly, when I brought her tea and fruit cake for her elevenses.

This morning I started on the living-room cupboards. John went into town on business, so Ethel, Jim and I enjoyed a workman's lunch of bread and cheese in the kitchen.

The bureau and the cabinet are also crammed with a jumble and I was back playing my hide-and-seek game with Aunt. From her bed, she could hear every move I made and insisted on the doors being wedged open so that she could see what I was up to. Now that she is feeling so much stronger, proud of surviving her heart attack and receiving good medication, she wants life to go on being lived her way. She does not really want this orderliness brought into her home, everything being made ship-shape, as if we are expecting an official visit from God in the guise of an admiral. She is hating her own common-sense decision to make use of me. I had come for a last farewell and to help bury her but now she is intending not to die.

By tea-time, I had finished clearing out all the drawers and discovered a nice little windfall, an uncashed pension cheque for $85.70, dated 1970, and also four gold sovereigns. I ran in to tell her that I had struck gold! "Finders keepers," she laughed and insisted on pushing the coins into my apron pocket — luckily not into the one with the matches for the bonfires.

We sat together, quietly enjoying tea and toast with Gentlemen's Relish, the early summer afternoon sun streaming in across the room. After I had cleared away and washed up, I came back to ask if there was anything she needed. She put out her hand.

"Come and sit here, close beside me, darling," she said and patted the eiderdown. "I want to hold your hand. All today you have been looking at me so oddly, as if there is something on your mind. I believe you are worrying that I am afraid of dying. I know that my time has come. What is death, if God lets it come to me so gently, at home in my bed with you children within call? I will simply be joining everyone buried in this valley, generations of our folk in the churchyards and all those generations under the Indian mounds. You remember that the Indians call those 'our old people', for their dead are really old. The trees that grow out of some of their burial mounds date them back over a thousand years ago. Their forefathers, the people who carved the petroglyphs near here, which experts date back to after the last Ice Age, may be 15,000 years old, or more."

How does Aunt still manage to think so clearly, with the precision of a governess (which she once was), putting all life into perspective? Are her faculties now freshly sharpened just because she is so near to death?

And so we sat together, the afternoon sun gradually slanting away across her room, the poplars slowly darkening on their northern sides, the bird-table deserted and only the hummingbirds still feeding from the aquilegia blooms, brilliant in the sun's last rays.

Her knowledge and wisdom all come from life, not from any higher education. Her schooling was just the three Rs, conscientiously mastered in a Somersetshire village schoolroom. I tried to thank her for all that she had given me since she and Uncle adopted me, for all that she had taught me as a small child.

"Your brain was so sharp that you were always in danger of cutting yourself with it," she laughed. "But you were a great dreamer too. You and John both used to daydream out of the window and you tried to fool me that you were just working out problems. Now my school in Somerset was a hideous, square, early-Victorian stone box and the leaded windowpanes were all set with thick lozenges of coloured glass so that we couldn't look out at anything. No distractions in that room and only sharp raps over the knuckles with a ruler to keep our minds from wandering away from the little bit of learning that we were getting. I suppose it was more than enough for most of the village girls, who were later going into service or to marry. It was the rector and his wife who encouraged me, he by letting me have the run of his library, and she through her belief in me. I never forgot what I owed them and we kept in touch until they both were dead – nearly 30 years ago."

And we talked about time: lost time, marking time, filling in time. Aunt said that she was especially happy because she had never wasted time. "I have lived it, lived every hour of it," she said, "and your mother did, too. That was one of the many things that bound us, from that very first day when we met on the deck of the ship which was bringing us both out west. She was standing quite alone, out of the wind in the shelter of a lifeboat, with a book in one hand, busily identifying the seabirds. As I came near her, she looked up, came over to me and said, 'I am Antonia Carfax', and gave me her hand. That was your mother – she looked you straight in the eye and gave a warm, firm handshake."

She went on to tell me that Mother was the first person whom she had ever seen dying. "I saw her soul leave her, long before she was dead and I held her hand and looked into a face which was only of this earth but not of her spirit. She had already started on another journey, the last of her 'travels'. You won't remember, but she was a great day-dreamer, too. Since that day, watching her die, I have never been frightened by the thought of death. As you get older," she went on, "you start to cast all unnecessary ballast overboard. I am like an old, unseaworthy hulk on its last voyage and one that is dragging out too long."

She had never heard of the pathologist, Virchow, but I told her that he had categorically denied the existence of a soul, because he had dissected the human body into the tiniest of pieces, right down to its most delicate fibres and discovered no trace of a soul.

"What a shock he will get when he dies," said Aunt. When I told her that he was already long dead, since the turn of the century, she just chortled. "Poor man! He will have had to swallow all his theories but at least he will have got used to the situation by now."

She is so full of surprises, suddenly saying that the proof of the existence of God lies in the fact that no one has ever been able to prove scientifically that He does not exist.

"You and Julian Huxley think along the same lines," I said.

John came in, then, asking for supper. I looked at my watch. We had been talking for over two hours.

But I never got around to talking about myself — which is, perhaps, a very good thing.

WEDNESDAY, MAY 17TH
(*Nearly midnight*)

Three days of concentrated effort and today, at last, the living-room is finished. The old furniture is beautifully polished, all the silver, brass and copper cleaned, and Ethel has had a field-day on the floor. John had taken the loose chintz chair- and sofa-covers and the heavy apple-green brocade curtains into town yesterday to Wai Tong's "Kwicky Dry-cleaning" shop, and while Ethel hummed and whistled her way across another of Uncle William's cedar-wood floors, I ironed in the kitchen.

The heat wave does not ease up and we had elevenses of cold mint-and-lemon tea with our biscuits. There is no movement at all in the air and the only sounds during the day were the whirring of the hummingbirds around the lilac and the purring of the aging marmalade cat, Higgins, now allowed to curl up at the foot of Aunt's bed. After a lifetime of being banned to the outhouse, he can't believe his luck.

We had a scratch lunch of cold meats and salad in the kitchen but I made some decent coffee with whipped cream. The coffee out here is awful – used dishwater! I had forgotten just how poor it is and I don't know what made me slip a couple of tins of "Viennese Mixture" into my suitcase. I think that all I am missing from Europe is the coffee – and the statue of the Empress Elisabeth in the Volksgarten in the centre of Vienna.

For a long time, I had been using the empress as my analyst to try to find myself again. I suppose that if I were a Catholic, I could have got help from a priest but I think people like me must learn to heal themselves. The empress listened in such an exquisitely detached manner. She never broke the thread of my thought, never impinged her own theories, but gave me all the time in the world to express myself and reorganize my ideas. With her marble hands lying gently folded in her lap and her far-seeing marble eyes gazing across the gardens, she helped me so much. She probably understands life's difficulties and passions far better now that she is a statue than she ever did in her own muddled lifetime.

I found her the day I visited Freud's old home in the Berggasse. The house was completely empty as I roamed around. I liked the atmosphere of his consulting-room on the quiet, courtyard side of the house. It was furnished rather like my memories of my great-aunt Agatha's Victorian mansion in the Cromwell Road in Kensington, but hers was crammed with vast mahogany suites, hunting trophies from India, antimacassars swathing every chair and a moulting parrot, older even than Aunt Agatha, and sleeping its life away, with one hating eye always open, in a corner of the unused library.

In that awful house, I spent the first ten months of my life in England, put safely in Aunt Agatha's care, before I escaped to a tiny attic room on the cheaper, northern side of Kensington Gardens. On my own, at last. Aunt Agatha loathed my Canadian accent, my independence and my "raw colonial manners", as she termed them, but most of all my student friends from the Slade. One day, she crowned one of her endless arguments with me with "You will end up just like your wicked mother!" and that remark drove me straight upstairs to the boxroom, to collect my trunk and to pack. This at least gave me time to calm down so that I was able to leave her house in a polite and civilized manner – but never to return and never to see her again.

And then dear Ilona Banat took me over. Yes, that is where she came into my life.

After I left Freud's house, I wandered up the Berggasse, crossed over the Ringstrasse, passing the bookshop, the coffee-house, the Burg Theatre and so in at the iron gateway which leads into the Volksgarten. And in there, behind a thick shrubbery, I found the Kaiserin Elisabeth of Austria, all in white, that superb horsewoman sitting as erect as in her saddle, but relaxed and in the fresh air, and I visited her from then on.

FROM HER DIARY

The calling of the owls, back and forth, from tree to tree, was keeping me awake, but now my eyes are very sleepy. Am I remembering facts or dreams?

Dr McKenzie called this morning. Aunt can now get up for an hour and then gradually increase the time each day. He had hardly driven out of the gate when she was out of her bed, despite protests, and demanding her slippers and warm dressing-gown. Her curiosity drove her as far as the dining-room and the living-room, while Ethel and I gave her two strong supporting arms.

She took everything in and was full of praise, except that she wants all the window-sills painted white. (The frames, mercifully, are lovely natural pine.) "They all look so scruffy, dear, since you had the curtains cleaned."

So that was today's job. I've done them all, cursing, with layers of the *Colonist* covering skirting-boards and carpets so that I did not ruin any of Ethel's good work or the freshly cleaned carpets. Of course Aunt is dead right. The new paint has made a world of difference. How wonderful still to mind so much about little things at that age, still to have an eye for detail!

By the afternoon I was finished – two coats – and so sick of the smell of paint that I borrowed J's car and drove over to the coast for a swim. Everyone thought that I was mad, to go swimming alone and in early May. The sea was still icily cold but marvellously clear and the shore utterly deserted.

There was a homemade raft, moored about 200 yards out from the beach and so I swam out to it, scaring away a group of well-fed seals and gulls who were enjoying a siesta. I wanted to rest on the raft in the sun, but it was covered in blood, fishbones and guano, so I just hung onto it in order to get my breath back and to watch some cormorants circling back to their young in the nests in the cliffs. Then I swam back to the shore. I must always have a target and swim flat out. I cannot just paddle around in circles.

Whenever I swim, I hear music in my head. Last Sunday, after church, people had said to me, "Don't you miss all the cultural things out here in the bush?" Thinking it over the answer is no! Not when I can have a swim like today's.

All the events which were once so important in my life mean nothing any longer. The many performances in the State Opera House, the Burg Theatre premieres, the Philharmonic concerts, these were all shared experiences. I always went with friends — or lovers. I scarcely ever went to anything alone, except to swim or skate, and so everything was affected by the current emotional waves flowing between us.

My early love for the arts and the little general knowledge that I first acquired came from all those evenings, first with Aunt Agatha in her box and then in the gallery at the Covent Garden Opera, or standing for hours of my young life at the Promenade Concerts in the old Queen's Hall, or perched in the galleries at Sadler's Wells or the Old Vic.

When one has stood for hours in a queue, usually in beating rain or in a chilling pea-souper fog, in order to get not a seat but a strip of hard board to sit on, the ticket-money always in lieu of a proper mid-day meal, one's critical faculties are sharpened to an intense degree, and so

is the ability to be transported, electrified. I have performances of Brahms, Mozart, Delius, Ravel, and Sibelius in my
head, and of Ibsen, Shakespeare, Chekov and Wilde behind
my closed eyes, the young Fonteyn, Ashton, Turner,
Helpmann, Markova and Dolin in my heart. A stockpile to
last me forever.

No, I am missing nothing, but I have a feeling of
drained, dry emptiness. I guess that I am simply pumped
out. It is good to lie like a bit of arable land, fallow for a
season.

FRIDAY, MAY 19TH

This evening, in the comparative cool, Ethel and I have
been cooking for the party which J and I are giving tomorrow evening.

Since we saw so many people at church last Sunday, the
news has spread along the grapevine that I am home again.
J had already invited a few people, just his closest friends,
but the phone has been ringing like mad all week and so
what was planned as a dinner-party for ten (and I think I
had a nice menu, simple to do – shrimp cocktails, roast
beef with garden vegetables, a lemon soufflé, cheese and
Irish coffee) will now be a cold buffet supper for nearly 60,
with a huge, iced, white-wine bowl.

Actually, that is far better, because it is too hot to cook
during the day and then play the cool hostess in the
evening. At breakfast today it was already 82° in the shade!
Many people wanted to invite me to their homes but I
turned down all invitations on the valid grounds that my
time here belongs to my aunt. "Oh! well, of course we all
know that you are now used to a quite different social life
over in Europe from anything we can offer you out here."

Touché! Everyone being over-sensitive and so, in order to avoid any ill feelings, we decided to have everyone come here.

So we have cooked, roasted, fried and baked as in the old days, sweltering but successful, not one of our culinary efforts either burnt or tasteless. It will be a fine spread. No fashionable caterers and hired waiters, serving epicurean delicacies on silver-plated dishes. No Vienna's famous "Demel" out here, but "Ethel and Claudia Limited" have done quite nicely, thank you!

SATURDAY, MAY 20TH
(*Two a.m. and in bed at last*)

All the guests have gone and we have even tackled the washing-up! It was a party for happy locusts – hardly a crumb left over!

SUNDAY, MAY 21ST
(*Sitting on the porch*)

After the late party, we had planned to have breakfast not earlier than nine a.m. but we all woke at the usual time. J had set his alarm clock since cows cannot be kept waiting, so I am resting on the porch and thinking over last night's success.

We had asked everyone to come around six o'clock and we had cleared most of the furniture out into the carport so that we could make Aunt Faith into the party's centre-piece. She held court, enthroned in the Queen Anne chair in the living-room, wearing her pretty, light-grey, gros-grain dress and her dark-grey satin slippers with the old silver buckles, loving every minute of it. It was just for an hour and then some young fellows carried her back to her bedroom. How she loved that – flirting all the way!

She was blissfully happy. Everyone came to greet her, kiss her, laugh with her and to congratulate her on the splendid recovery. It was a marvellous evening for her, for all her own generation have died, except for her old friend, Toby Welsh, now 96 and fading away in hospital in Victoria.

She has been a fixture around here for as long as anyone can remember and everyone has heard her stories a dozen times. She was always uncomfortably sharp with her observations, very much the governess and never suffering fools gladly. Now she is mellowed, sweet and able to listen to others.

It was so good to hear from all sides that I am looking not a day older and more beautiful than ever, even when it is not true. Now Mother was really a beauty, simply ravishing, but not I. Quite an interesting face, that's all. Everyone seems to have heard that I am very successful and I am congratulated on having made it in Europe. It is nice to be able to say that I also have two portraits in the National Gallery and one in Montreal. But there is no envy here, only genuine pleasure that someone from the valley has been acclaimed and recognized.

Most unexpectedly, J blossomed into a charming host and in his dark brown flannel trousers, royal blue linen shirt and a navy blazer with brass buttons, actually looked very handsome.

Lots eaten, lots drunk, and relaxed, amusing conversation about things like horse shows, sailing and fishing and holidays abroad, interspersed with women on their children, schooling, pottery-making and gardens. No one pretends. If you are talking to someone then they listen and look you straight in the eye, not like in Vienna, where they stare all the time over your shoulder to see if there could be someone more influential or more interesting coming through the door behind you.

MONDAY, MAY 22ND
(Lying in the hammock after lunch – 93° in the shade)
Yesterday was Whitsunday, when the Holy Ghost came to the disciples, bringing them three gifts – the gifts of tongues, of prophecy and of healing.

The gift of tongues – of communication – is not just a question of mastering foreign languages but of being able to listen to what is being said and then to reply to what has actually been spoken, not to what one would like to have heard. That has been my mistake in Vienna, struggling to learn yet another language, living in a strange environment and missing all the underlying subtleties of both foreign phrases and alien gestures. I was not listened to and I was deliberately deaf to much that I heard, for it was more comfortable that way. I needed no great gift of prophecy to foretell that my private life over there must ultimately be doomed to failure, however successful the professional one has been. I remain an emigrant because I do not want to be absorbed. I want to be known as a Canadian artist. To keep my own integrity. And so I am left with the third gift, the gift of healing, and that is being given to me only because I am now ready for it.

J went to church alone. I stayed home with Aunt and read the Bible to her and we talked about the meaning of Whitsunday, which sent me off on this track. I cooked lunch. Everyone is so surprised that I can cook at all and that I am domesticated.

For the very first time since I have been back home,

John asked me what my home in Vienna looks like, what sort of friends I have and how I live. Difficult to answer but it is nice to be asked, for he really seems to want to know. My home, my world? Where am I at home? Wherever I can fit my latch-key into a lock, open a door and there, in any four walls, I am at home. I've just added up that since leaving Canada in 1927, I have had 14 different homes in five different cities – London, Florence, Rome, Paris and now Vienna. J has never lived anywhere else than in this house, where he was born. Was I ever "at home" in the way J understands the phrase in any of these places? Perhaps in Florence. The eight years of study and work there, in my first studio, were very creative and wonderfully peaceful.

LATER, TEN P.M.

Thinking it all over, sitting up in bed, I believe that I have always been somehow homeless and restless. Toughness and obstinacy were the gifts given me at birth and a conviction that I would eventually make my way and completely on my own. I have always led the life of a gypsy and always been basically a nomad in a one-woman tent.

As a child, I remember saying so often to the grown-ups: "Oh! please do just leave me alone!" I was absolutely content just to have my dog, Goldie, and John for company, both of whom were silent companions. That was a wonderful childhood on this island, far away from any town life. As a child, I never questioned why we lived in the Cowichan Valley, by the lake; we just belonged there. Then, it was nearly an hour's drive in the buggy as far as the station, and at home, of course, there was no radio, televison, telephone or daily paper and in the evenings, all contours were softened by the light of oil lamps and wood fires. That childhood was the greatest gift that I could ever have been given.

But it was a tough life then – before, during and after the Great War of 1914–18 – always wrestling with the seasons; I was made to work very hard for my supper. My life has never changed and I am still working very hard for my supper.

Around midnight, someone at our party asked me, "How have you got all this marvellous vitality and this unbounded energy to do all you do at your age?"

What could I answer? It would have sounded ridiculously precious to have said, "Because I live in touch with the sun and the moon, with the spring budding, the warm late summer seas, the colours of the fall and the cold sharpness of the long winter," but it is true, and if one or two people can share certain moments of my life with me, then that is a bonus and a luxury.

I only want to paint. No thoughts, really not, of acclaim or of wealth. It is certainly very pleasant when one has extra money to spend but not of prime importance. Enough for care-free living and jam and butter on the bread. Ambitions? Yes, heaps of them for I want to paint better and make new discoveries. One is always learning, for one knows so little and the craft is so elusive.

Aunt Faith has the same strength, tapped from her daily contact with the land, and this has carried her on into a very old age, marred only by trembling hands and wobbly legs – and now this heart attack. She will never feel alone or discarded for she is sufficient unto herself and her example gives me hope for when my time comes – just around the corner now. She has never for a single moment wondered or bothered about what people were thinking or saying about her, nor expected any help. And so why should I?

I wonder if the art critics, the gallery directors, our small international circle of artists would stand by me with their help and their hot soup when I am as old and as frail as Aunt is now?

When Aunt called for me, I came. She did not know that she was tearing me away just at the height of my success, but I think, now that we have had the time to talk together so much, that she has rescued me from an empty life. I am sure that, all along, she has felt that I was just a homesick emigrant and, in reading between the lines in all my letters, that I was far too busy over-assuring all those back home that I was happy, that I was making it, that I had found many new fabulous friends and that fame and fortune were just ahead of me, to be reached along a rose-coloured, deep-pile carpet.

She called me back to where I belong, to discover the Indian summer of my life.

TUESDAY, MAY 23RD

The first mail has come from Vienna, including a letter from Director Braunsteg telling me that my *vernissage* was a tremendous success and enclosing all the press cuttings. They can be translated for Aunt without any censorship!

Twenty-three pictures have been sold, five before the opening and 18 during the evening and on the following afternoon. The director has given me the names and details of who bought what and why. We had firmly fixed all the prices before I left. Another five are reserved, including one earmarked for the Museum of 20th Century Art. Twenty-three out of 35 . . . fantastic!

It is so odd but I have the same feelings for each work as the over-anxious mothers at the balls of my youth, sad and hurt for the young thing who is not being invited by any boy to dance, but is bravely sitting it out, alongside her mother, at the edge of the ballroom floor. The paintings which are not purchased are truly my "wall-flowers". Why is one more upset by the sheer indifference to one work than thrilled by the laudatory acceptance of another? Why are negative feelings so much stronger than positive ones?

This afternoon, I made a new gauze fly-screen for the kitchen door, which seemed the right way to celebrate my success in Vienna.

WEDNESDAY, MAY 24TH

The old Empire Day and Queen Victoria's birthday. How dates stick in one's mind!

Over breakfast, J asked me very tentatively if I could possibly tidy up both his bedroom and the girls' old room which he now uses as an office and as a den for his record player and television set, both of which Aunt cannot abide and refuses to have in the living-room. They both come under her "over my dead body" pronouncements. He wants me to make suggestions about changing furniture or drapes. Nothing has been altered since Janet died.

When J and Janet got engaged, he and his father built these two rooms onto the west side of the existing house and extended the corridor on from beyond the kitchen door, so that they are linked to the rest of the house. The rooms are built up on stilts, as the ground here starts to slope gently down towards the lake and the low basement underneath is boarded in and used as a storeroom and general dump. It now also houses the new, oil-fired central-heating plant, although in winter Aunt always has a log-fire burning in the living-room.

The girls had sorted things out after their mother's death and so I actually only needed to put fresh lining-paper in the drawers and shelves and to lay a few clothes on one side for repairs.

Just before she died, Janet finished a thick, white candlewick bedspread and matching curtains and valances. Everything that she added to the comfort of the home is in good sound taste and planned on what we would now call "an economy budget", which then meant saving up every cent of the egg and cream money, turning frayed shirt-cuffs and collars, making false trouser turn-ups and unravelling and re-knitting shrunk pullovers and worn-out stockings.

I would not change anything in this room.

J has Mother's studies of water-birds on the walls and nothing else. Janet had the pictures perfectly framed in bird's-eye maple with a thin, gold inner frame to set off the subtle colours of the various plumages. Twenty water-colours all together, among them the Loon, the Scaup Duck, the Belted Kingfisher (one of her very best), the Mud-hen, the Maryland Yellow-throat, the Marsh-hawk, the Redbreasted Merganser, the Blue Heron and the Sandpiper, which we, when we were children, always called "The Peeps".

The strength of her compositions is that she painted the birds with the eye of a portrait painter. They are original – neither painted snapshots nor the usual accurate but rather sentimental "nature studies"; each is a portrait of an individual bird shown with a wealth of background detail in its particular habitat. I have never realized this before. She was a born naturalist.

When she first came out to Canada, Mother's early pictures were mainly the water-colour landscapes that are hanging in my bedroom in Vienna. She was still seeing everything through English eyes, making Constable landscapes out of our valley: not romantically idealized, never that, but typically English shapes and tones – nostalgic.

She left many sketch-books as well as finished watercolours and pen-and-ink drawings. She never had the money for oils and canvases.

Around the time that I was born, her style totally changed and she was painting the landscape as it really was – ruthless in winter, the desolate, craggy mountainsides, the impenetrable bush, the black storm-clouds mirrored in the treacherous, reedy lake. And she caught the gales blowing in from the sea and the heat and dust of parched summers.

Yesterday, after tea, Aunt was in one of her reminiscing moods and it was odd that she chose the old, old story of how Mother had once met Emily Carr. I think that I must try to write it down because it may be the last time she tells it and anyway I can't get it out of my mind.

"It was your Uncle Carlo," she said, "who influenced her so deeply to find a new style and approach to her painting, and who gave her the feeling that her work was worthwhile, but it was that chance meeting with Emily Carr that had the greatest effect on her, both as a woman and an artist. It all happened way back in the year 1895, long before Carlo came on the scene.

"Emily Carr was then living in Victoria and that summer, I think it was in July, she travelled up by train from Victoria to Duncan with two friends and from there, they set off on their bicycles for a sketching tour along the Cowichan Valley. Sometime during the afternoon, they stopped to sketch that lovely view across Somenos Lake. It was your mother who first noticed three bicycles leaning against the gate-post. Then she saw all three women sitting side by side on a fallen log, sketching in the shade of a willow, and so she went over and asked them to come for some tea. Everything that Antonia did was instinctive and spontaneous.

"After tea, the other two girls, whose names Antonia could not recall because they bored her, showed her the contents of their sketch-books but she was not impressed — their work was typical wishy-washy, amateur attempts and, besides, the girls chattered too much. But she was very attracted to Emily Carr, who just sat there — rather a mess and frowsily dressed, a plump girl with startlingly wide-set eyes under very straight dark brows — taking everything in.

"Only when the other two had gone out of the room to have a wash and to fix their hair, did Antonia ask Emily Carr if she might be allowed to look at her work. Emily showed Antonia the three sketches that she had done that day, all talented but rather conventional. Then she suddenly dug into her satchel and pulled out two other sketches and pushed them into Antonia's hands. One was of Indian canoes, moored in the rushes, and the other was a detail from a totem pole."

Aunt paused for dramatic effect.

"Your mother was speechless. Here was completely original work, nothing second-hand, just things seen with the strength of an outward eye, and, in the few minutes that they were alone together, your mother learned that here was another young woman trying to fight it out alone and go her own way as an artist. It was obvious that Emily Carr was not an easy person and that her way was not going to be plain sailing.

"Then the other two friends came back and Emily Carr quickly put her drawings away. They all said their *adieus*, as they wanted to get over to the Cowichan Inn, where they intended to stop for that night.

"And so the three cycled away and out of each other's lives. They did not keep in touch but later Antonia heard that Emily Carr had left to go and study in England. Antonia never left the island again, but now she knew that she was not alone in her attitude to her painting and that there was another woman, also alone and needing assurance and understanding, who already had discovered that an artist's path is a lonely and treacherous one. For nearly ten years, until Carlo came, Antonia kept all this to herself."

That is Aunt's tale of Emily Carr.

Mother never lived long enough to know that Emily Carr, that lonely and unhappy oddity, became one of Canada's most famous artists.

Was Mother a frustrated artist, her whole life simply mortgaged for us all? How shall I ever know? If only she had gone her own independent way, too. And what might have happened?

> If ifs and ands
> Were pots and pans
> There'd be no need
> For tinkers.

It is over 60 years since Mother taught me that saying and so I guess that she often took stock of her life – as I am doing, right now.

FROM HER DIARY

I'm writing all this sitting in Aunt's rocking-chair in the window, while Aunt is trying to sleep. She does not feel very well and for the first time has asked me to stay near her. J has just phoned Dr McKenzie and asked him to look in and to stop for a drink with us.

I am missing the European song-birds badly. The one-toned sparrows are quarrelling on the porch roof and the silent swallows are darting in and out under the eaves. It is so good just to sit and watch the world go by, the bird world – seeing, listening and quietly sorting things out and laying up treasures for myself.

LATER

It is talking about her beloved Antonia that so exhausts Aunt. I should not let her but I can never hear enough. Each word about Mother is so precious to me.

After Aunt finally got off to sleep, J and I went to look at the office room. It is just one big muddle and most gloomy, as the girls, years ago, had chosen a rather nasty yellow paint for the walls which has, with the passage of time, turned into a cow-pat brown. J is thrilled with my suggestion to paint the ceiling and walls white and also the window ledges, just leaving the door and the window frames their natural pine. We will go down to town tomorrow to buy paint and new brushes.

I am as excited about all this as if I were about to start sketching a new portrait. And why not that? What an idea! I have no paints here but I could buy some charcoal tomorrow and make a study of J for his birthday on July 3rd. That gives me time enough. I should, of course, be writing letters to Vienna.

Since I've been out here, I haven't written to anyone,

except a grateful thank-you letter to Director Braunsteg and a business one to the bank.

I'm keeping all my thoughts and plans to myself, hiding them away in this diary.

FRIDAY, MAY 26TH

Since Wednesday, I have slipped into a deep slough of depression and it is difficult to conceal my feelings from the others. I had not realized just how much I had been forcing the pace over the last months, living only on my nerves, on the capital, not on the interest. And it was an added strain to be so far away while waiting for the outcome of my exhibition, which had taken on such an importance in my life, quite out of proportion. Its success seemed to me to be my only justification for believing in myself enough to go on with my life. I had bet against myself — if I have a *real* success, then I'll go on. If not, I'll finish everything — which was of course idiotic. I would never have done it.

Now I have had a minor triumph and have to start to live all over again. Do I really want this sort of acclaim, now that it has come, and to be that kind of public figure? I honestly do not know if I ever want to return to Vienna at all. Do I belong there? Do I belong here?

And how long can Aunt go on living? Dr McKenzie said this morning, "Let her lead as normal and full a life as possible for she won't be with us much longer. She is made of grand old pioneer stuff but her heart got a real bashing."

This was a very clear way to warn us that each day may be her last. One knows it but cannot take it in. Helpless old age and death are traumatic experiences for us, the healthy lookers-on.

FROM HER DIARY

So, being in no bobbish state for making great decisions, I am just behaving like an ostrich, my head not buried in the sand, but bound up with an old scarf, while I furiously redecorate J's office and try to switch my mind off all my own problems.

J and Jim moved all the furniture out into the corridor and shifted the bookcases into the middle of the room, so that I can have a clear run with the ladder. I love moving along on top of it, its sides the extensions of my own legs; I feel like a real "pro" house-painter.

The great advantage of grooved wooden walls is that they need no repairs, not if built with first-class, seasoned boards and with Uncle Carlo's fine workmanship, and so the job has been fairly quick and easy. The undercoating was finished by tea-time yesterday and already the room looks much larger and lighter.

I feel a bit tired and dispirited to realize that my days up on a ladder do now seem to be numbered. Not that I openly admitted it, but the ceiling was rather trying. How lucky that I paint portraits and not church frescoes! But I suppose one could do a lot of that sort of work lying on one's back on a mattress.

This room is out of earshot of the rest of the house, and J rigged up a bell, so that Aunt can ring for me at any time, which has had the right psychological effect – she has scarcely used it. She spends her mornings in bed, gets up slowly for our family meal and then lies down on her bed again until tea-time, when J and I join her for her happiest hour of the day, when we all sit in the sun in her bay window, where she can enjoy the gorgeous profusion of the azaleas, rhododendrons and lilac and can give instructions to Mr Wei. Then she returns to bed. She never complains and spends most of her time reading – whenever she is not sleeping: at the moment, Pasternak's *Dr Zhivago*. She's full of jokes when anyone comes to visit her.

Quite a few of those whom we had invited to our party have since called in, just for a short chat. They have worked out a roster between them, so that she gets a visitor each day, which is all that she can cope with. Then I sit with them, over a cup of coffee or tea or a drink. They come because they are curious to see me, for they have not been near Aunt for years. I play second fiddle and they have to take me as they find me, as Ethel always says, and that is usually in paint-stained jeans.

Ethel is a great character. In the mornings, when we all gather for a cup of tea around eleven o'clock, Ethel is always the first to jump up, saying, "Well, luv a duck! Just look at that clock! This won't do to get married tomorrow!" and she scurries off back to her unfinished job.

Nothing more to note down tonight except a cricked neck, aching shoulder muscles and a beastly sense of insecurity and morbid speculations over my future.

At least I am sleeping soundly, so I won't complain.

SATURDAY, MAY 27TH
(*Sitting on the porch*)

The office room is finished! Although it was Saturday afternoon and she had a date with her sister, Ethel gallantly stayed and scrubbed the floor, which is just plain pine, and complimented me on being the cleanest workman she has ever had in the house.

J kindly drove her down into Duncan so she could be in time for the official opening of the new 5- and 10-cent store. This is a great local event and on no account to be missed as there will be free gifts.

J and Jim have replaced all the furniture. J will start to sort out his books next week and decide whether he needs more shelves. As he will be unable to part with one single volume, I reckon that he will need another 30 or 40 feet of shelving.

Another reckoning is that if I had left Vienna in my car, driven the 800 miles to Rotterdam and then taken the boat from Rotterdam to Montreal, which is a voyage of ten days, and then driven the 4,000 mies from Montreal to "Frome", I would probably have arrived sometime today – instead of three weeks ago. But I would have got here, just the same.

This evening, when helping to put the bookcases back against the walls, I saw Mother's Grieg album, lying among J's books on archaeological excavations. He has some fascinating books – among them, Howard Carter's three on the Tomb of Tut-Ankh-Amon; Davis and Maspero's works on the Tombs of Ioniva, Touiyou and Queen Tiyi in the Sudan; everything that he could lay his hands on in English about Schliemann's excavations at both Troy and Mycenae; Yadin's work at Masada and Hazor; Woolley's writings about Ur and dozens of books on Indian mythology which I have never read. I could live here for the rest of my life and never get through his library. That is one good reason for not returning to Vienna. After living 18 years there, I am within an ace of exhausting what interests me in the library of the British Council.

SUNDAY, MAY 28TH

Yesterday, the 27th, the Duke of Windsor died of cancer. It was announced from our local radio station. I thought of Benjamin Britten. He will have read the news in the Aldeburgh paper. It is the very first bit of international news that I have heard since I've been out here. Europe has just vanished off the map. We are as cut off here as they were in the pioneer times for we get only the news that the powers-that-be deem interesting for our consumption. And with frequent mail or train strikes, the post is often slower than it was when I was a child.

Anyway, British Columbia is busy with other matters. There was a big parade in Victoria last Monday to celebrate Queen Victoria's birthday. Last night, the Cowichan Indians performed their Indian opera, "Tzinquaw" ("The Thunderbird"), in the school hall.

I saw the last performance, which they gave years ago! It has taken them all this time to get around to reviving it. Time, for the Indians, is wholly relative. That performance was so gripping and impressive in its simplicity that I have retained the evening in my storehouse, for all time, and did not go to last night's revival for fear of ruining a flawless memory.

I will never forget the sound of the drums, heralding the burial procession, nor the great contralto aria of grief and mourning, with its bursting crescendos and sudden pianissimos, as the old woman turned away from expressing the public mourning, the ritualized tribal show of sorrow and sank back into herself, into her own private, agonizing bereavement. This aria ranked with Kathleen Ferrier's farewell to Eurydice, in that last and unforgettable performance of her short life, on the stage at Covent

Garden Opera House. Ferrier was then already in touch with death herself. The Indians live, as we all should, hand-in-hand with both life and death, the coming and the passing of our earthly span.

The Indian singer's name was Syvestre Modeste and I will never forget her voice for as long as I live. Modeste and Ferrier.

LATER, IN BED

We were walking slowly back from church and had just reached the upper pasture, filled with cornflowers, aquilegias and light- and dark-purple spotted orchids, when J suddenly stopped in his tracks and asked me if I would marry him.

I burst into tears.

"What an utter fool I am to have asked you at all!" he said. "Just because I am so lonely and you are such a darling person. What I have to offer you — well nothing, bloody nothing. It may have been a damned poor idea of mine but surely nothing to make you hullabaloo about? For Heaven's sake, dry up, girl!"

He was quite knocked out by my reaction. How could he know just how confused I have been feeling? So, after I had mopped up, cleaned my glasses and blown my nose on his handkerchief, I put my arm around his shoulder and said, "Please keep the offer open, Johnnie dear, if you can. Will you forgive me?"

So we kissed each other on the cheek and left it like that — for the time being. I am completely *"bouleversée"*. For all these years J has been my young brother. I helped change his nappies, taught him to fish and to skate and to ride a bike. He learned on the one that Uncle William gave me before J got a proper boy's bike of his own. And I helped him with his homework and was sister-bridesmaid at his wedding and then godmother to his girls, to both Celia and Joanna. This has been my role, all those years. For nearly 40 of them I have been writing home to Aunt, always with a special extra message for J, and we wrote to each other for every birthday and Christmas.

Aunt does not miss a trick and thought that we had had a row but we managed to laugh off her remarks. Tonight, my little concert for Aunt did manage to restore the old atmosphere and both J and I were happy and relaxed again. I played my favourites out of the Grieg album: the "Tableaux poetiques op. 3" and then the "Notturno op. 54 no. 4" and then some Debussy for J, "Images".

Mother was with us – I felt her standing right by me. Am I really heading for a collapse? Mother never knew this house. It was designed and built after her death. How can she come back to a place that she had never seen in her life-time? Of course, if you believe a simple idea of an after-life, Uncle William could most certainly have told her all about it.

I simply can't accept that this sort of phenomenon is only our wishful thinking and that we project what we want to see and to hear. Why should that traffic be only one way? Why should not the projection come from Mother's side? If she adored me as much as everyone has always told me that she did, she must want to follow my progress through life, to keep in touch with me in her way, letting me know that she is near.

For I *know* that she was there. Had she come to tell me something? Was it the Grieg that brought her back to me?

Only about five or six times have I seen and felt her and, when I come to think it over, always in moments of indecision. Only long afterward I have realized that her visit had coincided with a turning point in my life. Not that I ever had the feeling of being given a push from behind — rather of being drawn very strongly by her in an unknown but certain direction. It seems that at these moments of indecision, one is particularly receptive if one remains absolutely still, a waiting blank canvas.

TUESDAY, MAY 30TH
(After lunch, lying in the hammock)

The heat wave continues — 82° in the shade at breakfasttime! The wisteria over the porch has surely never been so loaded with blossom nor so alive with bees.

I had the feeling that J avoided me all day yesterday and he disappeared soon after supper to sort out his books. I have made a circle around him too, as I have to give him an explanation and an answer. Actually, I have always loved him.

First in my life was, of course, my darling Mother and then there was just nothing, a terrible emptiness, until John was born. For years, I thought he was a present from Mother, sent through the post, because one morning Uncle Gerald called me in from the yard and said, "Claudia, a wonderful and very special present has just arrived for you!" It was Mother who had always given me presents and so of course he was from her.

About a year later, there was a second special present, my very first puppy, the Labrador "Goldie". I found him tied to our gatepost by a string. Uncle Carlo told me that it was his "goodbye present" to me, but I knew that Goldie came from Mother, too.

So I focussed all my passions on those two – John and Goldie.

J has always adored me. For him, I was the person who could do and show him everything. He trusted me completely and trailed around behind me; with him and Goldie in tow, I fished and swam and sailed and went off for hours on end, with my drawing things and a bag of apples or some cookies for us. J was never in the way, always a book in his hand and always happy. I was his "Claudie-crony", as he called me then, and Goldie was the important third in our inseparable trio.

Suddenly I have re-entered J's life as someone who can cook, clean, carpenter and cope generally. I am a going concern and also a woman who still has a good figure and even a glimmer (on good days and with my back to the light) of sex appeal.

Back here again, I know that I have allowed myself to soften, to laugh and to feel again, and of course it makes all the difference in the world to express myself in my own inherited, rich, English language, after all these years of Italian, French and German. Now I realize just how much I have cut myself off from my Cowichan Valley roots and from the culture here, both native Indian and imported European.

But I am still so restless and I don't know why. Shall I stay on here with J? Take the line of least resistance? I think that I cannot go back to living in Vienna. I don't want to go on working in that studio. The city has outlived its purpose in my life. That is the important decision that I have been able to make. I want to make a completely fresh start and in a positive atmosphere. The good friends will remain but many will drop me, and, in some cases, I guess I will be grateful. It will be a healthy weeding-out process. I am spring-cleaning my whole life, tearing up, throwing away, making bonfires.

It is strange but from where I am lying in the hammock, I have only just noticed that all the swallows have disappeared and their nests under the eaves along the south porch are deserted. Not a sound. What can this mean? I feel that this is not a good omen, a worrying thought.

LATER THAT EVENING

This afternoon I drove into town and fetched all the wood which I will need for the shelves and the window seat. As I had taken my scaled plan with me, the carpenter, Jack Willans, very kindly cut the wood into the right lengths for me; this will save so much time as J has only hand-saws. Jack Willans was at school with me, nearly 50 years ago now. He still has reddish hair and a squint.

Tomorrow I will do all the carpentry work so that when I leave here, at least I will have done my best for J as well as for Aunt. I can do no less and that is pathetically little in exchange for all that they are giving me – without even knowing it.

THURSDAY, JUNE IST

Today came a cable from Director Braunsteg with the news that the Museum of 20th Century Art has purchased the reserve portrait. This has capped my success! Also, two others have gone to my American agent for American collectors.

But the window seat was very tricky to mitre. However, in the end, it all fits together beautifully. I am rather proud of the job and J is so pleased. Ethel has volunteered to make seat-cushions to match the curtains, which are a most unusual and attractive design of delphiniums. The designer must have been a keen gardener for there is the gentian, (Agnes Brooks), cobalt, (Blue Brilliant), indigo, (Blue Tit), a rich violet, (one of the Langdons), silvery-mauve, (Silver Moon) and a sky-blue, (Betty Hay, perhaps?). Ethel says that the original material is still obtainable at the Hudson's Bay Store in Victoria and she always knows what's what.

The room is so light and orderly now – a happy one.

Could I ever make J happy? We are still skating around each other, on alarmingly thin ice, exchanging small talk and platitudes.

This afternoon after tea, we helped Aunt along the corridor to show her J's finished room. She found it a great improvement. We drank a glass of sherry to toast my latest success and then we steered Aunt happily back to her bed, rosy cheeked and sparkling. She is blessedly happy and I wonder, suddenly, if she has put J up to the idea of asking me to marry him?

I am so safe here with the family. Life is launched daily on that body-building breakfast and the day's work is planned and tackled with quiet optimism and the feeling that all will go well as everyone is doing his best and, if things don't work out quite as one had hoped, then we'll make light of it. We have enough to eat from our own land, the well is deep and never runs dry, there is enough cordwood stacked up to dry for the next winter. Our corner of the universe is in halcyon order.

Tonight, Aunt asked me if I would look at the basement under J's two rooms and sort things out down there. "There is the church's summer bazaar coming up early in July," she said, "so we can get rid of the things there. If you phone the rector, he will get the Scouts to collect any goods in a truck." She thinks of everything.

So, with my mind off Vienna, off J's proposal, off all future plans, I will get down to the basement, first thing tomorrow after breakfast! I have decided to give myself a target. When that job is finished, the last of the dirty work, I will give J his answer. Definitely. I must give myself a time limit to end all this vacillation.

IN BED AT 10:30 P.M.

I am so wonderfully sleepy. It is probably the direct result of switching over from Austrian coffee and Scotch whisky to China tea and Canadian rye, and to hell with the psychology!

FRIDAY, JUNE 2ND

What a junk-heap that basement was! In the first and larger one, where the oil-heater stands, I salvaged three bicycles, an iron clothes' mangle and a suction cleaner. It is the great-grandfather of the modern vacuum cleaner but it works like a concertina, breathing in the clean air and puffing the dirt into its metal container. Underneath coats of grime it is a blazing, pillar-box red, glories in the name of "The Monarch Cleaner" and weighs a ton.

Then there were over 300 flower-pots in every imaginable size. Mr Wei has picked out the best to keep for our own use. Then there are 38 large panes of glass from a long-dismantled greenhouse, and yards and yards of old drain-piping and guttering, replaced years ago by tough plastic, and then boxes of jam-jars and bottles.

But the real prize was an old "His Master's Voice" gramophone, complete with soundbox, wooden needles and a red and green horn. There was a mildewed case, containing a mixed pickle of records, Charlie Kunz at the piano, the old Savoy Hill Dance Band, a medley of Gracie Fields, lieder boomed away by Clara Butt and then that celestial boy soprano, Ernest Lough, singing "Hear Ye, Israel!" from Mendelssohn's "Elijah". I must have brought them back with me from London, on a visit sometime in the early 1930s.

At the back of the basement were three huge rolls of rat-eaten felt under-carpet and enough chains to fetter a galleon full of pirate cut-throats. Whatever were they used for? Also hundreds of coloured glass bottles for pickles and preserves, some now museum pieces which fetch quite a few dollars in the antique shops at Whippletree Junction. There are also many articles to be sorted out and then carefully stowed away again – packets of good roof and wall shingles, coils of rabbit-wire, rolls of tarred roof-felting and lots of fence posts, all cut and trimmed.

My favourite useless find was a sound lavatory bowl, stamped:

THE STORM KING
LUTON
BEDFORDSHIRE

Oh! it was a grand day of running to the window to tell Aunt of each new find. I was far too filthy to come into the house and my elevenses and lunch were delivered to me on a tray to the cellar door by Jim.

Praise this heat wave, because I could pull everything out onto the grass and so wash and clean each article in the fresh air.

The basement slopes back from about six feet in

height at the door to only about two feet at the back so it is very tiring and difficult to work in, especially because of its dusty earth floor; I kept hitting my head on the beams.

Tomorrow I will tackle the inner basement. There does not seem to be much there as the roof is so low, but three or four suitcases or boxes are jammed in, right under the back wall, so I will have to crawl in and drag them out with a hook on the end of a rope.

On Sunday, I will have absolutely no excuse not to talk to J. My time-limit will be up! The best moment will be when we are walking home from church.

SATURDAY, JUNE 3RD

The very last thing I hauled out from the basement was an old suitcase. When I opened it up, I discovered layers of ancient, rat-nibbled curtains, but in one corner, there was an unlocked, rusty deed-box. In it, I found a collection of letters with a note on the top of the first envelope, in Aunt's handwriting, saying "Only for Claudia".

I took the box straight to my room so that I could examine the contents later, when I was quite alone. Tonight I went off to bed as early as I could, pleading tiredness, and opened the first bundle.

The letters were tied in small bundles, with rotting ribbon, and arranged in chronological order; the first letters were all from my Grandmother Newton-Lanes to her son, my Uncle Wiliam. I had no guilty feelings about reading them for they do not belong to either Aunt or John.

Then came Uncle William's letters, written home to England and most of them still in their envelopes, such tiny envelopes. All have two-cent stamps with old King Edward's bearded head and, later, the two-cent stamp of the young George the Fifth. Uncle's letters are written on very thin writing-paper and his writing is cramped and most difficult to decipher. He wrote on both sides of nearly transparent sheets, trying to squeeze in all he could on each page, and with a quill pen. Grandmother's letters, on the other hand, are all clearly and boldly written, flowing over expensive stationery.

I have not told either Aunt or J that I have found these letters, not yet. Maybe I will first read them all and then slip them back again into the deed-box, to lie for another 50 years in the cellar behind the oil-heater.

LATER — 4:30 A.M.

I have read all the letters. Oh! my poor, darling Mother! How much I now understand.

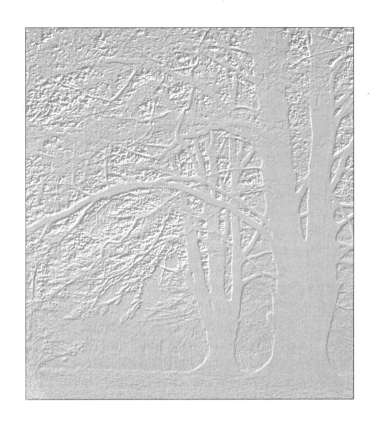

PART TWO

WILLIAM'S STORY
– *The Letters*

INTRODUCTION

I HAD NEVER SEEN or heard from my English grandparents, Mr and Mrs Newton-Lanes, for they had both died when I was a small child, living on Vancouver Island. By the time that I left the island to travel east to study in London, I only found their graves, in a sadly overgrown churchyard. That was all I knew of them. But I could imagine the scene so well, for I had been shown many family photo albums when I was living with Aunt Agatha.

The Newton-Lanes family had lived for many years in the Cheshire countryside, in a large stone mansion set squarely in a walled garden, where very little grew with any colour in it. The main features were four huge oaks, some laurel bushes and a weedless drive, which swept one in from the country lane, through iron gates and across to the flight of eight entrance steps to the porch. Then it curved away to disappear towards the coach-house.

After reading the letters, I could visualize the scene in the dining-room, dominated by a huge oval mahogany table, which could seat ten on the matching hand-carved chairs with padded leather seats . . .

On a January morning in the year 1909 only four chairs were occupied – by Mrs Newton-Lanes, her husband, her younger sister, Miss Bella Woodhouse, and Mrs Newton-Lanes' companion, Miss Sutherland. They had just finished a nourishing north-country breakfast. Miss Sutherland was asked to pull the bell to summon the parlour-maid to clear the table. Mr Newton-Lanes, who had been securely isolated behind the pages of the *Manchester Guardian*, got up to open the door for his wife and then disappeared into his study with the newspaper and his portion of the first early-morning post.

Mrs Newton-Lanes went slowly upstairs, alone. The chill was now off her sitting-room, as the coal fire had been burning for over two hours. She unlocked her marquetry bureau, chose an envelope and two sheets of notepaper from the second-best quality and, after staring out into the misty garden, where the rain was dripping off the old oaks, she started her first letter to her son, William, in Canada . . .

"Oakleigh"   (*undated*) January 1909

My dear Son,

Yesterday evening your Father brought home the good news that you will be docking safely in New York harbour tomorrow. He had had to go into Liverpool on urgent business, and took this opportunity to enquire at the shipping agents. It so happened that Mr Clarke was in his office down at the docks, and so your Father was able to thank him personally for his truly kind and inestimable help in obtaining that deck-cabin for you, at the eleventh hour. Of course, we are very fortunate in that both your Grandfather and Father have been important shareholders in the shipping firm for well over seventy years, and that your Father has been active with his legal advice in so many ways. Undeniably, the world being as it is, this does make a great

Mrs Newton-Lanes

difference when one is suddenly put into the uncomfort-
able position of having to ask such a favour.

Your Father arrived home on foot, frozen and soaked
to the skin, right through to his Jaegers. He had ordered the
station cab to meet his train but it was not there. Instead,
Mr Payne himself was waiting for him on the platform, full
of apologies, to explain that his mare was out of action.
She had slipped on an icy road earlier in the afternoon and
was badly strained.

The weather has been simply bitterly cold since you
left us and the barometer is nearly always at "stormy". I do
not like to think of the weather which you will have had at
sea. I can never forget being a witness to the appalling loss

of the ship, *Eurydice*, with over 300 men aboard, in that terrible gale off the Isle of Wight, when we were there on holiday in the Spring of 1878.

Of course, it would have been a far quicker voyage to Quebec and Mr Clarke said that he could easily have procured a first-class single cabin for you on April 3rd, when the first ship leaves port this year for Eastern Canada. The Canadian ice-breakers will have opened up the sea-route by then but, so I understand, it was not possible for you to delay your departure any longer. Our thoughts have been with you on this very long voyage and we can only hope that your cabin companions were quiet and amiable.

I am still unable to take it all in. Everything happened so quickly. I can see you, going off as usual after breakfast to the Bank, (or so we thought), and then came the arrival of the police, enquiring as to your whereabouts and your Father and I completely baffled and utterly at a loss. I do not know how I lived through those few days until your departure from this country. However, your Father and I have decided never to refer to the matter ever again, neither to each other nor to the family, and certainly never in our circle. It is now a closed chapter and we ask you to respect our wishes in this matter, completely. You may consider me to be a very hard woman, but I have been brought up to live my life dutifully, fearing God and upholding my station and the morals and standards of the society into which I was fortunate enough to be born.

We have decided to inform any enquirers that the reason for your sudden departure was to take over a property, left you in the Will of a distant cousin of your Father. We have given the matter a great deal of serious thought and prayer and have decided that this explanation is compatible with our consciences. After all, we hope that you will indeed be able to purchase a piece of land one day and start farming on your own over there. Your Father has set his heart on this project and you just cannot let him down again.

As you well know, it was only his personal appeal to the Magistrate who was hearing your case, and his own position as a Justice of the Peace, which saved you from a prison sentence and made it possible for you to be given this opportunity of making a fresh start abroad. Now it is up to you to make the very best of this last chance and to prove yourself to be a man.

These are my final words on the subject.

Your Aunt Bella joins me in all good wishes to you for your future in British Columbia. I think that she is starting one of her feverish colds. She went out for a long walk yesterday with your dogs, in such stormy weather and wearing the most unsuitable shoes.

Ever Yr. affec.

Mother

"Oakleigh"   (*undated*) January 1909

My dear Son,

Your cablegram sent from Ottawa has just been delivered. Now you are crossing the continent. Our thoughts are with you on this long train journey which, unfortunately, you must undertake at the most inclement time of the year.

We had a blizzard here yesterday and it is icily cold. Your Aunt Bella is still in bed, enjoying her ill-health. Your Father is also confined to his bed. He succumbed to a very nasty bronchial attack, with accompanying high fever. This is, of course, the direct result of that day in Liverpool on the draughty docks, all his anxieties on your behalf and also getting so soaked on the return journey home. Dr Martin is calling daily and is, so far, satisfied with the progress being made by his two invalids.

The Rector also called, interrupting a most pleasant tea-party which I was giving for Lady Wetherington, Mrs Knott and Miss Arrowsmith. We were just discussing whether we should engage a man to come and paint all our greenhouses in the Spring. The Rector stayed for less than ten minutes. He left an invitation to a lecture on the works of Mendelssohn, to be given by our organist Mr Mankey, next Tuesday evening. We all four expressed our willingness to attend and our interest in the subject of the lecture. He left three more invitations for my guests. I trust that, by then, the ice and snow will have melted so that we will be able to go in our carriages, otherwise I shall stay at home, sending my regrets.

Several people in the village have asked after you and I was very pleased to be able to report that we had had your cablegram from Ottawa. One does not know just how much people may suspect and facts are always satisfactory. This village is uncomfortably near to Manchester. I carry your cable with me in my handbag, ready to show to any-one who might enquire about your whereabouts, and, principally, to scotch any rumours. It is difficult to ascertain just how much of this tragic and sorry affair has become public. The realisation of the difficulties, not to mention the deep sorrow which your immoral actions have inflicted on your entire family, is only now beginning to be comprehended. Our prayers were never said with such heartfelt emotion. You can make a fresh start. We have to carry on with our daily lives as before, but now living under the shadow of your shame.

Ever Yr. affec.
Mother

"Oakleigh"   4th February, 1909

My dear Son,

The last of the snow has melted and the roads are free and dry again for the carriage traffic. It has indeed been a very long and tedious Winter, made even harsher for us through the recent events and also through your Father's illness.

The Bronchitis developed, alas!, into Pneumonia and Dr Martin was very worried indeed and called three times daily. However, his patient has responded to the treatment and nursing very well. Tonight, on leaving us after his last visit, Dr Martin remarked to me, "Mr Newton-Lanes is my very favourite patient and I simply cannot do enough to help him to get fit." How lucky we are to have such a conscientious young Practitioner in our village!

The maids have kept very busy, tending the fire in your Father's room, night and day, but they are devoted to him and are as relieved as I am that the corner has now been safely turned. Miss Sutherland has been a tower of strength to me. I do not know what I would have done without her constant support. She is by far the best Lady Companion whom I have ever engaged.

Last Wednesday, your Aunt Bella recovered enough to be able to lie down on the day-couch in her bedroom for a few hours and, when Dr Martin called later in the afternoon and said that she might go downstairs, she went at once. Her recovery has certainly eased the work for the staff, which has had to cope with not only the fires and meals on trays for two invalids, four times daily, (your Aunt's appetite is never lessened), but then, of course, our regular household meals and their normal duties. Illness in a house is no excuse for not doing one's work properly.

Your Father has so many friends who have called to enquire after his well-being and always at times when one must offer either morning coffee, afternoon tea or Sherry and biscuits in order to be civil and hospitable.

All this worry brought on my usual Neuralgia but my good friend, Miss Arrowsmith, gave me her very simple prescription, which has already worked wonders:- 1 oz. of Grains of Paradise, ½ a pint of Gin. Stand for 24 hours. Squeeze a flannel out in the solution and apply to the affected parts. Such a useful remedy and so I am sending it on to you.

Your train will shortly be nearing Vancouver, so your Father informs me, and so you are very nearly at the end of your long journey. It is very difficult for me to imagine the great distance that now separates you from your home, and for ever.

Ever Yr. affec.
Mother

My dear Son,

The afternoon post today brought a most welcomed and reassuring letter for your Father from your sister, Antonia. It would seem that, on receiving your Father's cablegram last month, George started to build a room for your use onto the west side of the house. I cannot imagine that it will be ready in time for your arrival, nor how George can build anything at this harsh time of the year, but your Father informs me that if George has enough seasoned timber already cut and stored, and can get some help from his neighbours, then there will be no difficulty in building a small room in the time at his disposal. For once in his life, George seems to be acting quickly and practically, which is hard to believe.

Antonia is happily looking forward to your arrival and to hearing all the latest news from the Old Country. She will never admit how homesick she must be, nor that her very hasty marriage to George was the catastrophic mistake that I felt it to be at the time. To have made his acquaintance in a railway waiting-room, and then to have become engaged and married and sailing off with him to Canada, and all within less than a month, not only broke my heart but also boded no good for a well-founded marital future for her. The ingredients for a housemaid's novel are not the proper constituents for a durable marriage. You were far too young at the time to realise just what a deeply sorrowful time that was for your Father, for us both.

However, it was indeed an ill wind that blew good for you, my dear Son. You will not be alone out there but have the support and experience of your Sister to help you in building your own future. Antonia possesses a very strong character indeed.

Now I will close my letter with the words of the Bishop of Lincoln, which were published in our Parish Magazine for February, and which are very relevant to your present situation:- "Let us speak what is given to us in all simplicity and be ready for corrections: what matters is that we be teachable to the end and faithful to our trust".

Ever Yr. affec.

Mother

The Fens,
Duncans,
Vancouver Island,
British Columbia,
Canada.   6th February, 1909

My dear Mother,

At long last I am here! I arrived at "The Fens" yesterday afternoon and had a most truly warm and loving welcome. George came alone to meet my train at the local station and drove me up, with all my trunks and boxes, in his roomy farm-wagon. They did not know just how much luggage I would be bringing and so he came alone, to leave all the space for my things.

His neighbours, Mr and Mrs Aitkin, were up at the house waiting for us, and also Miss Faith Meare, (who helps with the children and the household), and, with Antonia herself and the two children, I was given a truly magnificent "Committee of Welcome", with toasts and appropriate speeches all round. After about an hour, the guests took their leave, knowing how much family news we had to tell each other. Most tactful of them.

Everyone looks very well and supremely happy. The house is really a splendid one, what is called a "frame building", with a large bay window to the sitting-room, looking across the garden, now covered in deep snow. Everything out here is built of wood, all the windows have cornices and the ground-floor rooms on the south side all open out onto a broad, fretworked verandah. The rooms are most comfortable and very pretty. Antonia has made a lovely home here for George and the children and with such good taste. She has quite a few old things from her rooms at "Oakleigh". I remembered the charming little Davenport writing-desk, the Buhl cabinet, where she now keeps all her music, and the upright pianoforte, with its swivelling brass candle-holders and the brass pedals.

And can you believe it – they have built on a room specially for me! I am simply charmed with it. It is splendid to have a room of one's own, to feel a member of the family and not just someone extra in a guestroom. George has built it with a corridor between the house and my room, so that I have my own entrance and front door, opening out onto the back garden and the end of the hen-run.

Antonia helped me to unpack last night, after supper, and we sat for hours on my bed while she asked me a thousand questions. It seems that Father in his letters had told her nothing, so I told her just everything. I found it so easy to talk to her. I thought it was up to her to decide whether to inform George or not, but she thinks it wiser for us to keep our secrets to ourselves. She is a grand woman and even lovelier than I had remembered. I was only a little lad when she came out here and she did not recognise me at all when I came up the garden path to the house. It was so amusing!

Everyone is delighted with the presents which you gave me to bring out to them and very touched by your thoughtfulness. Miss Meare was especially moved by being included in the list of recipients. Thank you once more very much for thinking of just everything that I could possibly want out here. George was amazed that Father had even thought of a gun, fishing-tackle and waders, and those magnificent long leather boots are the envy of all beholders. The real prize was the "Home Pharmacy" and the children have already christened me "Uncle Doc"!

Charles and Claudia are both very good-looking children. The boy seems to be most well-mannered and is very tall for his fifteen years. The little girl, who will soon be three, is very like her mother, with almost black hair and very dark-brown eyes, wide-set in an ivory face. A striking child. She immediately attached herself to me and climbed up on my lap to hug me, to the amazement of everyone as she is normally very shy. She is a deep one.

After breakfast this morning, I swept my room and made my bed and helped with the washing-up. I am learning. George and I then sawed timber from fallen trees for firewood. The tree was about 200 years old so you can guess the size of it. George is a dour, humourless fellow and difficult to get along with, so I was indeed glad when lunch-time came. However, on the walk back to the house, he told me how he and Antonia first met, quite by chance, on Crewe railway station, whilst waiting for two quite different trains. "It was 'Kismet'!" he said, so surprisingly. Perhaps I will gain his confidence in time and I will certainly do my best to be very tactful and not get in his way whilst I am living in his house.

Everyone else is easy, kind and helpful and the place had a fascination for me at once. Already the past seems to be far behind me, almost as if it had never happened, and sharing it all with Antonia has made it so much easier for me. She is a wonderfully understanding and very broad-minded woman.

Antonia and Mrs Aitkin are driving down to the village this afternoon with the horse and buggy to post letters and to purchase a few things from the store. Duncans is really only a huddle of wooden buildings – a general store, a bank and post-office and some single-storied homes, grouped near the railway halt on the single Esquimalt-Nanaimo line which goes down to Victoria. This halt was the end of my 3,000 mile train journey across Canada.

Here, the weather has been very wet indeed and I was kept from coming earlier by a bad wash-out on the line. It still looked very unsafe to me when we passed over what looked like loose planks but I did get here and all in one piece.

Antonia is calling. I must stop. I will write to you regularly each week. Please give my love to Aunt Bella, my kind regards to Miss Sutherland and to the maids and to old Sykes. My best love to you.

Ever Yr. affec. Son,

William

Antonia has just suggested that we all go to Church tomorrow to give thanks for my safe arrival.

William Newton-Lanes

The Fens, Duncans.   14th February, 1909

My dear Mother,

I have now received your two letters from January and will respect your wishes. I will never refer to the past again. It is now locked away and no one will ever find the key.

I am so sorry that Father is ill and hope that he is now very much better. One feels so cut off out here, with the mail taking between three and four weeks each way. Antonia says that you can tell down at Duncans, when the mail train comes in, just how long someone has been out West. There are those who can hardly wait to get out of the mail office before tearing their letters open, and then there are the old settlers, who stuff their mail into their saddle-bags and ride silently off home. I am in the first group.

The weather has been pretty severe since I came. We still have very thick ice on the lake and it snowed again last night – about eight inches, not too deep, for which we are grateful, but enough to prevent us from driving to Church. We tried to get there on foot – it is three miles away, along a trail through the bush, (as forests are called here), but we gave up after half a mile as it was too much for the children. So we returned home and read the Bible together, seated around the dining-room table, taking it in turns to read the verses.

Since I last wrote, I have done up my room. It looks very smart. The walls to a height of about six feet are stained like oak. Really it looks very nice. Antonia got a second-hand large chest-of-drawers from Victoria when she went down this week with Mrs Aitkin. I scrubbed it out very thoroughly and put it by the stove in the kitchen to dry and then painted it light green. Very fine it looks and now I have completed my unpacking and all my gear is stowed away properly.

George has been away all the past week as he has got a new job, working on a survey at a place called Goldstream, about thirty miles south from here in the direction of Victoria. The atmosphere at home is so different when he is not here. He puts a damper on everything.

There is a young man living quite near to us in a shack on George's land. He is a bachelor like me, but quite a bit older. He lives off odd jobs. His home is like many around here, built of rough lumber and roofed with shingles. He built it himself. His name is Carlo Ghirlandi and he helps here quite a lot, especially when George is away. Originally he came from Italy, from somewhere in the hills above Rome, and is a nice, agreeable sort of chap, very handsome. As he is now busy making a new hen-house for a man in Duncans, he has been away every day this week and I have been pretty busy, trying to do all the odd jobs. Carlo does the first milking before he leaves and Antonia has taken over the second milking, which she enjoys. It is so restful to think like a cow for an hour or two, she says. She can turn her hand to just anything.

The house has a milk-cooling room, where she also stores her jams and jellies, preserved fruits and a large keg of cooking molasses. Every household here is self-supporting and only flour, tea, salt and sugar are brought up in bulk by train from Victoria and carefully stored. She also keeps ducks and mixes their mash with a huge, beautifully carved wooden spoon, which an old Indian woman gave her as a present when Charles was born.

She told me that when they first came out here in 1890, there was only a handful of people settled in this long Cowichan Valley. The early pioneer homes are cabins, built of peeled cedar logs, with a cedar shake roof, a fireplace of local stone and a privy on a path back in the bush. A long way from the comforts of a home like "Oakleigh"! Some homes here are now empty and falling into pieces, which is sad. It seems that quite a few men had enlisted for the Boer War and have never returned. Some had not really made it out here or thought that they would try their luck elsewhere, far away from this lonely bush land.

Now I will try to give you an idea of a day's work here:- I rise at 6.15 a.m., light the stove, wash myself, make a cup of tea and then walk over to Carlo's place to call him.

He sleeps like a dozen logs and he asked me if I would do him this favour. Then I take up tea to the ladies. This is my little treat for them, as neither Antonia nor Faith have enjoyed this small luxury since coming out to Canada. I wish your maids could see me!

Then I get the porridge on and take up hot water for the ladies' baths. We have two wooden hip-baths and I carry the water up in the set of eight brass water-cans, which Aunt Bella gave Antonia for her wedding present. Do you remember them? It is enough for a splash. Meanwhile I go to the cooling-room and draw off the milk from the deepsetter, scald the deepsetter and prepare the milk and oilcake for the calves. Then I cook the bacon and make coffee for breakfast. Then comes breakfast – my favourite meal of the day, and we all have it together around the big dining-room table. Then I wash up the breakfast things with Faith. (Please do not be shocked. Everyone is called by their first name, no "Miss" nor "Mister" out here.)

Then I lay the fire in the sitting-room, chop firewood and bank the fires during the day. I then clean the stables (every day) and the hen-house (twice a week).

Faith calls us all in for morning tea at 11, which is a happy and welcomed break. Then different jobs till lunchtime at 12:30. Antonia is a marvellous cook. Then we wash up the lunch things and I do other jobs, like sawing firewood, filling in holes in the road, mending fences, felling trees, sawing up trees in order to roll them out of the bush etc., until tea-time at 4 o'clock. Then the deepsetter again, feeding the hens, ducks, cows, calves and horses and bedding them down etc. Supper is at 6:30 or 7 o'clock. Then wash up the supper things, chop wood for my stove in the morning. Eight o'clock is reading and music, (Antonia and Faith both play the piano very well – Antonia solos, Faith prefers duets), or we simply sit and talk by the fire until 10:30 or so. Then bed.

Saturday night is bath night for the men, in front of the kitchen fire in the warm. Everyone gives us a wide berth and no callers are allowed! This is an established custom out here.

I am hoping to hear that Father is better. Please give my love to Aunt Bella and my kind regards to Miss Sutherland and the maids and Sykes and to any friends whom I still have. Next week, we are starting to lay a road and clear some land that Carlo is buying off George. I think it only fair to help him all I can as I have found out that it was actually he, and not George at all, who built my nice room, but George takes all the credit for everything around here and we just let him blow his top off. Anything for a quiet life. I have no more news, so goodbye. My best love to everybody.

Yr. affec. Son,

William

This is a grand and beautiful country and I am so excited at being out here. It is now Sunday afternoon and we are all writing letters in different parts of the house – Antonia is upstairs in her room and Faith and I are sitting with the children. George has not come home, so they must be snowed-in down at Goldstream. Carlo has just tramped over to join us. We are a merry party and full of fun. Carlo sends his kind regards to you, and Faith does too. Before I forget, could you most kindly send the *Athletic News* out to me? I miss the reports very much and Faith's fiancé, Gerald Carruthers, would enjoy it too. He was a great cricketer (in

Sussex), it seems, before coming out here to try his luck. What a completely different life I am leading out here! You would not recognise me.

The Fens,
Duncans Station,
Vancouver Island.   14th February, 1909

My dearest Papa,

Today I am writing my usual Sunday letter to you but sitting upstairs in my room, alone. Usually, we are all gathered cosily around the fire in the sitting-room, but I do not want William to see what I am writing. The room is small when we are all in it together. He has been here a week now.

The evening that he came, he unburdened himself to me and told me the whole story, very frankly, very honestly, holding nothing back. The sea voyage in this winter weather must have been awful, a nightmare, and he was going over the events again and again in his mind, knowing that nothing he could ever do would put things right again, especially with you, his adored Father. He showed me the letter that you had written to him to the boat, "To be opened only on the voyage" and, after I had finished reading it and had folded it back into its envelope, he took it out of my hand and without waiting for any comment from me, he burnt it, then and there, in his funny dramatic way, slowly watching the paper blacken and curl into the fire. Then he simply said, "That's that, isn't it, Antonia?" We have never referred to you nor to your letter again.

Mr Newton-Lanes

I think I know why you do not want to hear from him nor wish him even to send a greeting through me. He told me that he had started a long *mea culpa* to you, even before he had left home, and continued it on the train to the docks, but then threw it overboard. Thank God that I am here to help him and that he now has someone to whom he can talk. I promise you faithfully that I will take care of him, dear Papa, as you have entrusted him to me. He gets on very well with all the household, loves his bachelor quarters and seems happy enough, especially with the children, who call him "Uncle Doc", because of his marvellous medicine-chest.

His accent is very "Oxford" and he carries himself far

too elegantly for life in the bush. I am not so sanguine about him getting work: manual labour, I mean, as I was. You see, Papa dear, he has never had to do any at all before and, although he is very strong and healthy through all his sport, he is very very slow over everything and, at his age, it seems almost impossible that he should or could easily learn to do things with the smartness of men who have been accustomed to manual labour from their youth. He could, I should say, easily make his living by some sort of office work but that he seems to dread, does not wish to discuss it and becomes positively wrought-up if you press the idea. As I now know what happened back at home, I understand his feelings. At the present, he seems contented and very wishful to help in every way, has laid down a "Daily Work Plan" for himself and so aspires to please, that I could not for the world hurt his feelings by hinting, even, that he will have to learn to do jobs a thousand times quicker before he can possibly get work of any kind outside. Please do not mention this to Mother nor to anyone else. As you well know, in some ways William is really painfully sensitive and needs very careful handling.

He wants to write to Mother every week. That he wishes to maintain some contact with home, I understand, and as he and Mother have never been really at all close to each other, it will be easier for him to write a weekly account of his life over here to her and so preserve for himself at least an illusion that he is keeping in touch with a home and a land to which he can never return. He has still not taken in the reality and seriousness of his situation. One day he will have to face up to facts.

We have all been grieved to hear how ill you have been, Papa dear. I am so very very sorry. Now you must regain your strength so that you can get out again for your long walks when the warmer days come.

I must stop now and make some scones for supper.

How typically generous it was of you to insist on paying for the building of the extra room for William! Please do not mention it to anyone else, but I have given the money to Carlo, who actually did the entire job himself, except for some help from an Indian lad, who has already been paid for his work.

As long as William lives here with me, he can easily manage on the monthly remittance that you are sending out to me for him. I will try to save as much as I can of this money in order to help him in the eventual purchase of his own piece of land, which I know is your dearest wish.

With a very great deal of love to you and all good wishes for your speedy recovery. Please do not worry anymore. Just consider your own health. William is safe here, with me.

Always, dearest Papa,
Your very loving daughter,
Antonia

"Oakleigh"   21st February, 1909

My dear Son,

At last the snow has melted and we have warmer days, but your Father has not yet dared to go out. However, we have had a surprise which has been far better than any doctor's tonic. Your Brother, Arthur, was in London all last week on business and returned home on Friday evening to inform us that he has been promoted to assistant manager in the firm. We are, of course, simply delighted and very proud of him. His progress since his brilliant final examinations has been almost meteoric, and your Father sees a solid future ahead for him. You will realise just what this means to us at this time and, I hope, rejoice with us. He is everything which a son should be, except that I am still not happy about his marriage. He could have done so much better for himself instead of marrying into that very bohemian family of journalists and artists. I am only glad that I insisted that Olivia should come to "Oakleigh" for a month before their marriage, so that she could at least learn from me how a household should be properly run. She proved to be surprisingly amenable. Your Father says that she has an angelic nature.

Last week, your Father seemed so much better that your Aunt Bella and I were able to drive over for Mr Mankey's second lecture on the composers. Owing to your Father's illness, I was unable to attend the first lecture on the composer Mendelssohn, but received a very favourable account of it from not only Lady Wetherington and Mrs Knott but even from Miss Arrowsmith, who fancies herself as something of a musician, having studied the pianoforte under Mr Zeper, the Dutch pianist.

The lecture was given in the village hall and was very well attended by everyone of note and also by many of the villagers. As organist and choir-master, Mr Mankey has, of course, come in contact with the entire church-going neighbourhood. He chose to lecture on the symphonies of Beethoven. Beethoven was born in Bonn on December 17th 1770, which was also the date of my dear Grandfather's birthday. Such an interesting co-incidence.

Beethoven having composed nine symphonies, it was a

Mrs Newton-Lanes at a children's croquet party, with William second from left and Arthur on her lap, both boys dressed like little girls, as was the custom

very long lecture and time running short, Mr Mankey decided to save Nos. 6, 8 and 9 for a later lecture, which will also include Beethoven's operas, "Leonora" and "Fidelio", which are two versions of the same story. He says that he will also touch on "Egmont", "The Mount of Olives" and also "The Ruins of Athens".

The lecture was richly illustrated by Mr Mankey and his daughter, performing on two pianos. It was only a pity that, with her unfortunate complexion, Miss Mankey chose to wear a gown of shot purple taffeta.

Last week, we engaged a Mrs Mulcahony as cook, to replace Annie Kirk, who has gone to live with her married daughter in Scotland, near Inverness, which move I know that she will later regret. Here she had an excellent wage, (it was raised a shilling a week only last December), her full board and lodging, a uniform and her own room, and we always gave her a week's holiday. She having been with us for over twenty years, the kitchen and the staff were completely under her control and many perks came her way, as our numerous guests are always very generous. She will not enjoy the role of mother-in-law in another man's house.

Mrs Mulcahony came to us with excellent references from her previous employer but he must have been only too thankful to be rid of her. She is so dirty and extravagant that she will be leaving us at the end of the week. Luckily, Miss Sutherland's aunt has died, quite suddenly, and her cook will come to us almost at once. I do not know what I would do without dear Miss Sutherland's support.

Your Aunt Bella has been under the weather but is taking a new mixture of Phosphorus and Nux Vomica to rouse the torpor of her nervous system. She joins me in good wishes to you and also Miss Sutherland and the maids and Sykes all asked to be remembered to you. No one else.

Ever Yr. affec.

Mother

The Fens, Duncans.   21st February, 1909

My dear Mother,

Carlo has made a little Indian-ink sketch of the house for me to send to you with this letter, so that you can visualise how we all live. He is such a kind fellow and, as you can see, a really gifted artist. I enjoy his company very much. He tells me that the porch and the front of the house are pretty in Summer, when the climbing roses bloom, (Paul's Scarlet and a Lemon Pillar and an Emily Gray), and the honey-suckle, (Early Dutch), and two magnificent Nelly Mosers climb right up to the gable. The large flowerbeds under the windows are a mass of Lupins, Canterbury Bells, Larkspur, Delphinium, Arnica, Mrs Sinkin's Pinks and Californian Poppies. It is nineteen years since they moved over from the mainland and George and Antonia found this heavenly spot and sank all their capital into what was then only bush and marshland.

For Antonia, from the beginning, it has been a never-ending struggle under what we would consider the most primitive of conditions. (You see it all in her hands, thickened, the skin broken and the joints rheumaticky, like a road-mender's.) I think the flower garden is her greatest joy. The bulbs will be up soon. The fruit and vegetables are a close second. All the wives exchange plants and cuttings, compare notes and give each other gardening tips. In fact, the whole way of life out here is different to England – co-operation and not competition. People may be curious about new-comers, which is customary, but there is a natural reticence. No questions are asked and no information is expected. You can keep as much or as little of your past life to yourself as you wish. It is the only means of survival and, for people in my sort of position, a blessing. Everyone's door is open, too, or the key hangs on a nail where any chipmunk can find it.

Carlo told me that when he came to these parts, five years ago, he discovered Antonia's encyclopaedic knowledge of ornithology and her great need for solitude. So he made a path, partly on duckboards, partly mounted on wooden stilts, through a corner of the marshes where the vegetable garden ends. It leads to a small landing-stage, which he also built for her. Here she keeps a rowing-boat tied up, round-bottomed and with a small storage cuddy forward. In the late Spring and in the Summer months, when she is missing from the house, you may be sure that she is hidden somewhere in the marshes, studying the bird life. She comes back with lovely drawings in her sketch-book, which she works at in the evenings. I have seen some beautifully detailed Studies which she has drawn of the Eared Grebe, with its glossy black neck, its upright pointed helmet-like crest and its cheekily smooth face. It nests in large communities in the marshlands but does no damage. Do you remember that Aunt Bella once had a very smart Sunday hat which her milliner trimmed with the plumage of a Grebe? Antonia's latest Studies are of the Marsh Hawk, resting on a rotting tree-stump by the water's edge and another of one in flight. It is like a lightly-built Buzzard as it beats up and down the marshes, searching for prey — mainly mice.

Our social life centres around the Church service on Sundays, when one meets everybody, exchanges news and gives and receives invitations for the coming week. The main topic now is the rehearsals for the amateur theatricals in aid of the Church organ. We are giving two one-act plays, entitled, "Cool as a Cucumber" and "The Coming Woman", both produced by the Church organist, and he has cast me for a small part in the first play.

The biggest event for me is, of course, the arrival of the train. On Saturdays, I try to finish my jobs early, get washed and generally cleaned up and ride down in my best togs to have a beer in the saloon bar of the inn, which is directly opposite to the Halt. Coming up the straight track, the train-driver sounds the steam-whistle almost the entire time in order to scare any straying animal off the track and so you get a fair warning. As it nears the Halt, a bell is rung continuously until the train pulls out again. It is a red-letter day for me.

Vaccination is the other topic of conversation with us all just now as there have been a few mild cases of Smallpox in the district, among the Indians only, but everybody is being vaccinated as a precautionary measure. There is not much danger of it spreading among the white people but, sadly enough, several Indians have already succumbed to it. They are very susceptible to all European illnesses. Charles and Claudia were done a fortnight ago. All the children here were treated first. Charles had a bad arm. It had taken splendidly and he felt quite ill for three or four days. Claudia took it all in her stride. Then Antonia, Faith and I were done but so ineffectively that we had to be re-vaccinated today. Carlo, too, and his arm is very bad and he feels pretty seedy, poor fellow. Luckily George has returned for the weekend and has taken over the milking. I am still rather slow at it and need more practice. George gets very impatient with me but the poor cows put up bravely with my fumbling efforts. Everyone sensibly keeps out of the way while George rants and curses, which helps neither me nor the patient cows.

I wish that you and Father could look in some evening and see us all gathered around the fire, each with his or her special chair, reading papers or books. Antonia has promised to sing for us tonight, including two of my favourites, "An die Musik" and "Der Musensohn". It will be a Schubert evening. She has a lovely soft alto voice.

No one knits or fidgets and all chatting stops when she plays or sings for us. You would be pleased to see what a harmonious party we are! On Sunday afternoons, we all sit around the dining-table to write our letters home to the Old Country, under the light of an adjustable hanging lamp, filled with what is here called "coal oil" and what we know as "kerosene". It is fetched up from Duncans, where it is delivered in five gallon cans, two rectangular cans are contained in a strong wooden case. I took three of these cases, did a bit of carpentry on them, painted them green to match my chest-of-drawers and now I have a fine cupboard for my boots.

I am so looking forward to the arrival of the first number of the *Athletic News*. I do so hope that my old Lacrosse team, with Arthur now as its captain, will get into the finals which must be nearly due to take place. How I miss the sport, and my dogs!

Everyone is very busy making toys for Claudia's birthday, which is next Friday. She will be three years old. I am such a duffer at carpentry, I have discovered, that I will bake her a box-full of sugared Noah's Ark animal biscuits, like old Annie always made for us boys at home, when we were about Claudia's age. Do you remember? I was never allowed to try my hand at cooking. It was Annie's domain, but I did watch her at it.

My best wishes to all at home.

Yr. affec. Son,

William

The Fens.   28th February, 1909

Dear Aunt Bella,

I was very touched to hear from you and to feel that, in spite of all I have done, which may have damaged the family name, you have not cut me off. Your letter has meant such a great deal to me. I can admit to you just how much I miss you all, my home, my friends, my team and the dogs. It was truly kind of you to write that you miss my cheery laugh around the house.

Perhaps you will be interested to hear an account of my adventures yesterday. For the first time since I have been out here, I gave myself a "half-holiday" and felt just like a schoolboy again. I thought that I had earned one and I badly needed to get off on my own.

Behind our house and across the valley, there is a high, rocky, square mountain that has fascinated me ever since I came. The Indians call it "Skeecullus" or "The Sad One". The family has never been up it but I felt that, after Snowdon and Ben Nevis, I could easily tackle it. So I took George's mare and set off along the valley on a well-worn trail, bordered by willows, hickory and witch-alders. Suddenly the sun came out very strongly and lit up a twisting line of shale at the foot of the mountain and leading away from the creek at the water crossing. I had such luck to spot this trail through the pines.

The curious thing out here is that you are somehow so much more aware of *single* things – just the shape of one pine-tree, a lonely cricket chirping, the swish of a grass-snake. I did manage to reach the summit, foot-slogging it for at least a third of the trail. Leading the mare, it was a fearful struggle, so I decided to tether her to a very curiously-shaped tree, which I knew that I could locate again, and actually I was able to keep it in sight for the remainder of the steep climb. This is not a country in which to have an accident nor in which to get yourself lost.

The rocks at the summit are worn completely smooth and flat, exposed as they are to all weathers. The view is superb, so I sat down and looked across the Cowichan Valley and over to our lake. I even thought that I could spot Faith, (Antonia's friend who helps in the house and garden), in her bright blue working-dress, feeding the chickens. I could see as far off as the broad sunlit line of the sea, separating us from the mainland and from the snow-covered range of the Rocky Mountains, over which I crossed only three weeks ago. Only three weeks!

I stayed up there for over two hours. I needed time to think, to be quite alone. For the first time since coming out here, I was aware that I have left your comfortable world and my former easy life forever – completely behind me. That life is all finished for me and there can be no return. You see, both the voyage and the long train journey were somehow utterly unreal. Always surrounded by other passengers, sharing a cabin with three businessmen and my sleeper on the train with a chattering farmer, I was allotted the role of the adventurous new settler and played up to the part as best as I could.

In those insane days in January, I acted like a hunted animal and was deservedly cornered and killed. I lost my head. If I had been a Catholic I suppose I could have gone to confession and perhaps some good priest would have given me absolution and guidance, perhaps have even gone with me to the police, before I gave in to being blackmailed by that fellow in Liverpool.

But the Anglican Church leaves you very much alone with your conscience and your personal God. I sat up there on those rocks just thinking and thinking it all over and over again. I do not know how much Father may have told you and I have promised Mother never to mention the past, but I feel that I must ask you for forgiveness for any pain or difficulty that my rotten actions may have caused you. Please forgive me, dear Aunt, for I am so fond of you. Now I have Antonia to help me to start a new life and she has understood and accepted this odd and forbidden side of my life.

I will never go to that mountain again. It is haunted and not only in my imagination, by silence. There are no song-birds out in these parts. At least, not as we know the orchestra of bird-song that we experience in England, and I felt shapes pressing around me, heard sudden crackings of twigs in the bush, a glissando of shale, but there was no one there. I felt that I was trespassing – worse, that I was somehow desecrating this mountain peak by my presence there. On the way down and when I was almost at the river-crossing, I suddenly heard the sound of an owl, right above my head in an arbutus tree. It went on calling, calling after me until I was over the crossing and had turned a bend in the river and was out of ear-shot. I suddenly felt very cold and shivery. It was nearly dusk. I will never go that way again.

This is a funny sort of letter and perhaps I should tear it up but, apart from the daily round, the common task, there is little to report. Well, we have all recovered from the vaccinations and are busy. All ailments are treated very perfunctorily here. There is no time for ill-health and to be laid up. Remedies are simple – bread poultices for abscesses, mustard plasters for chest complaints and Castor Oil and Senna Pods are the mainstay. Mother would heartily approve.

Mother wrote in her last letter that you are up and about again, which is good news indeed. I am worried about the dogs but I am sure that if Father is still bed-ridden, you are looking after their welfare, but promise me not to exercise them yourself in bad weather and so get ill again! I know that you love the dogs almost as much as I do and will see that they get enough exercise. How I miss old Sheppy! Rufus too of course! When I get a place of my own, the very first thing I will do is to get a dog. I have not seen any Old English Sheepdogs out here. I must enquire. How far away you all seem to be — and, indeed, are. My fond love to you, my dear Aunt, and please write again.

Ever Yr. loving Nephew,
William

"Oakleigh"   1st March, 1909

My dear Son,

Your first letter from "The Fens", dated 6th February, has just come with the morning post. How thankful I am to have it and for the account of your safe arrival and of your first impressions of your new home! So, George did get the new room built in time! I never expected it of him, I must frankly admit, and I am more than agreeably surprised. I am also glad to hear that all our gifts were acceptable. I knew that a pair of double Whitney blankets would be the right present for Miss Meare, for her "Bottom drawer", and I am glad she is pleased. Doubtless

I will be hearing from her. She seems to be a very good friend of the family, in all respects.

It gladdens my heart that Antonia has become a Church-goer. Probably the responsibilities of marriage and the children have made her realise, at last, that true help comes only from on High. The Churches of the Anglican Community are a centre of spiritual Faith in this heathen and materialistic age. You may not realise that the Mother Church of England has planted Churches not only in Canada, but also in Rupertsland, India, South Africa, Australia and New Zealand and is closely associated with the Episcopal Church in the United States of America and even with the Church in Haiti. There is much external evidence of the unity of these Churches, exemplified by the Conference at Lambeth, in which the Bishops of the different Churches meet together and where that most important function, the Episcopal Succession, is continued. You, my Son, also have a part to play, albeit insignificant, in this great Community of the Faithful. No sinner has ever been turned away.

Your Father has ventured out of doors again and has even taken a few short walks with the dogs, who seem delighted to be with him again. Their favourite walk is along the Upper Canal, where the tow-path lies on higher ground and it is always the first stretch of path to drain dry. He must still be careful. Aunt Bella accompanied him on the first walk, but he prefers to go alone, that is, of course, except for the dogs.

We are expecting the first of our many visitors at Easter, when I hope the Spring weather will help to make their stay a pleasant one, and so we are starting the Spring-cleaning earlier this year. Five slates were blown off the roof in the last storm and two gutters broken, so Crossfield's men are here to make the necessary repairs. We have also decided to have new grates fitted in the drawing-room, library and in my sitting-room. This was long over-due. It is no use to start the cleaning until all the workmen are out of the house. All this work will leave us with only the dining-room heated, where the grate is in excellent condition and drawing very well.

Therefore, your Father and I have decided to go to our usual hotel at Buxton Spa for three weeks. It always does him good there and we can both take the waters and, as guests of long standing, we always receive admirable attention.

We have recently accepted invitations from our circle of close friends: lunch at the Sissons' and also at the Hewletts', lunch on Sunday, after Mattins, at the Rectory and also a very pleasant tea-party at Lady Wetherington's, where we also found Sir Rupert, the Rector, Mr Blain (the Duke's bailiff) and the four Wetherington daughters. All four unmarried and their situation not likely to be altered.

The man has just come to paint the greenhouse. I have got him to do ours first and then he goes on to Lady Wetherington.

You may remember that we purchased a new kitchen stove from Fenton's store in Lancaster, last October – "The Mistress Stove No. 8"? We had much trouble with it and have at last discovered that it only burns satisfactorily on Long Arley coal. Fenton got the stove for us from Carlisle, I now hear, and had simply no idea what fuel was suitable. On what type of stove is your cooking done? Do you have much trouble in obtaining fuel? Here, it is always a problem, even if you order in good time. We have just had a truck of coal delivered from Pope and Pearson which should have come last month. Most unreliable of them!

Aunt Bella sends her good wishes to you. She has been suffering from a pain in her side and ordered a "Durlow Magnetic Belt", which she saw advertised in a magazine. It arrived today, with the parcel post. I doubt if it will help her.

Miss Sutherland wishes to send her kind regards and the staff always ask after you. Your Aunt will take charge of all the Spring-cleaning in our absence.

Ever Yr. affec.

Mother

CABLE

Addressed to:- Arthur Newton-Lanes, Esq;
Dated:- 19th March, 1909

ANTONIA PASSED AWAY TODAY AFTER SERIOUS
OPERATION STOP PLEASE INFORM OUR
PARENTS STOP LETTER FOLLOWS STOP ALL
HEARTBROKEN STOP
GEORGE AND WILLIAM

The Fens, Duncans.   21st March, 1909

Dear Arthur,

I thought that the best thing to do was to send our cable to you, at your office, and George, for once, agreed with me. I knew that if we had sent it to the Parents, they would have been simply stunned and quite helpless, especially Father. As you know, he simply adored Antonia. We are both aware that we put a very heavy load on your shoulders but I am sure that you will have coped wonderfully, in your usual calm and efficient manner. I am very conscious of the fact that you and I parted company only a little over two months ago, in an atmosphere of intense hatred and bitterness on your part, but this is no time for personal differences. George has already written to the Parents and I understand that he is also writing to you tomorrow.

The tragedy has been terribly sudden. Poor Antonia complained of a pain in her chest, only about ten days ago, and went to see our local doctor. After examining her, he said that she must be operated on in Victoria as soon as possible, and he fixed everything up. Four days ago, Carlo drove her to the Station and she went down by train and was operated on the next morning by the surgeon, Dr Thomas, a very clever man, by all accounts. He found that it was a large carcinoma and had to remove the whole of one breast and a lot more. It was an entirely successful operation at the time, but a clot of blood formed and she passed away quite suddenly and quietly and without any pain. The doctor says that the condition would most certainly have occurred in some other part of her body for she had left the operation very late. So she might have died

Arthur Newton-Lanes

suddenly at any future time. Faith, who went down with her and who was with her before the operation and at her bedside when she died, told us that she never regained consciousness, which was indeed a mercy.

Carlo and the boy and I were all at home but, of course, had no idea of the fatal issue of the operation. None of us realised that it was so serious. George was down at Goldstream on the survey job and so the moment we heard the news from Victoria, we cabled for him to return home at once. (Mrs Aitkin had very kindly taken care of Claudia until Faith got back.)

The funeral took place today. It was a lovely sunny day. She is buried at our Church, under an old oak tree. She had always wished to be buried there. The service was very beautiful but inexpressibly sad. We sang her favourite hymns, "Abide with Me" and "Nearer my God to Thee".

George and I, Carlo and Gerald (Faith's fiancé) carried the coffin. Charles did not go as we thought it would be too much for him at his age and so he stayed at home and looked after Claudia. There were hundreds at the Church. It was simply crammed. Everyone was mourning her departure from among us.

I am afraid all this sounds very incoherent but I feel too stunned and sad to write any better, any fuller. She had a glorious smile on her lips – a completely peaceful expression. She was such a dear good and most beautiful woman. Oh! God, I cannot write any more or about anything else. My heart is too full.

The Parents will perhaps feel it all even more than I do. They have had so much trouble with their two elder children. I suppose it was God's Will but it seems very hard.

Ever Yr. affec. brother,
William

The Fens.   Sunday 4th April, 1909

My dear Mother,

It is three weeks since our darling Antonia left us and, as yet, no word from you. I hope for a letter soon and then I will answer immediately, as you will surely have asked me many questions.

I am more than glad that we decided to send our cable to Arthur. We did not know that you were both in Buxton while Father recuperated after his illness. This news only came in your letter of the 1st March.

We are a very sad household, everything about the

place reminds us so much of her and I realise now, more than ever, that all our lives revolved around her. She held us together. The Wednesday after the funeral, we all went to Holy Communion. A very beautiful service it was, too, with special prayers for her soul. How much I miss her and, without her encouragement, I find the life over here very hard. And I thought that I was a fit man and tough.

George has been home ever since she died. His job at Goldstream was finished anyway and Mr Harris, the chief surveyor, had paid everyone off. He was indeed very lucky that this good job had lasted almost two months. I expect that they will be starting another stretch of the road soon. I do hope so and not only for his sake. George is not an easy man to have around, day in and day out. Faith saw through him years ago and there is no love lost there on either side.

All weekend, we have experienced the most awful hullabaloo from George concerning the Will and he is going down to Victoria tomorrow to consult a lawyer. He is absolutely furious and is threatening to contest it. Luckily neither you nor Antonia had ever taken me into your confidence over such matters so that I have been able to remain strictly neutral.

Of course I never knew that Father had purchased this property for Antonia and George, nor that he had given her the money to build and furnish this house. It came as a great surprise to me to hear that the ownership of the property is legally registered in your joint names. Knowing George as I do now, I appreciate how wise it was of you to have tied up the property in this way. As I understand things, he will only inherit a joint tenancy with Charles, at your deaths, and that I and Carlo are the two trustees until

Charles reaches the age of twenty-five. Antonia's Will states that all the furniture and her personal possessions etc. are to go to George, apart from a few personal bequests and that, on your instructions, the lawyer has told Carlo and me that we are to be allowed to continue living at "The Fens" either for as long as we wish or until the death of George or until Charles reaches the age of twenty-five. I foresee great difficulties for both of us and the situation may be very unpleasant.

Well, we can only wait until the Will has been proved and then we shall know just where we all stand. How I loathe all this and how possessions only corrupt us all. By the way, Antonia had few personal possessions and there is no jewellery left. All her good things were sold long ago, piece by piece, to pay for George's "extravagancies" – Faith's expression.

Carlo avoids George completely, except at meals, but in any case he has been away every day, making "broody hen cotes" for Ken McIntyre and tomorrow he goes down to Duncans to make new chicken runs for the Mortons. He is the crack carpenter of the district and can always get plenty of jobs.

Antonia's death has upset us both very much but we are trying to keep our minds off our great loss by plenty of hard work. Carlo and I have ploughed, sown with oats and harrowed two acres of our high field. Since then, I have been busy sawing and carting stove-wood. Two of our hens are hatching and we already have twenty-three chicks. The hens are not laying well, but I expect that we shall have a perfect glut of eggs soon and then we shall crock them for the Winter.

Gerald and Faith have managed to buy twenty-five

acres and we are all going to work together to build them a house. They want to be married as soon as it is ready. Faith promised Antonia that she would stay on here to look after us until she marries and she is managing magnificently. It is so much work for her but I am trying to help her all I can, even with the cooking. My experience while camping-out on walking tours now comes in very handily.

I am always thinking of you all and long to see you again. I am very much alone now, in spite of everyone's great kindness to me. All our neighbours have been so thoughtful and truly sympathetic. They are really good Samaritans, all of them. I think there is not a single family near us who does not in some way miss Antonia. How much she concealed from us all! I often wonder now if she knew that she was so ill. The doctors say that the cancer would have recurred and that it was a merciful release but it seems very hard. She would have been so pleased to see the improvements that we have been striving so hard to achieve. I am sure that it will make you happy to know just how much she loved this beautiful home and treasured the property. Her one sorrow was that you and Father had never seen it all. I shall continue to write every Sunday but I fear that my letters will be a poor substitute for dear Antonia's.

Ever Yr. affec. Son,
William

My dear Mother,

Firstly, thank you so much for sending all the papers. The most interesting, for me, is the *Athletic News*. My heartiest congratulations to Arthur, as the new captain of the team, on winning the Cup! Through all our recent sorrow, I have forgotten to send any message of good wishes to him on his appointment as assistant manager in his firm. I know that what I think or do is totally without any interest for him, but I am so glad that you have at least one of your three children of whom you can be truly proud.

I did not thank you for the two pairs of pyjamas. They are so warm. We have to wrap up well at nights. In fact, despite all precautions, we suffer very much from rheumatism. I suppose it is caused by the damp marshlands.

George is off on survey again, which is a great relief. He came back from seeing the lawyer in Victoria on Tuesday and was off on Friday, in a filthy mood. It seems that the Will is clear and all the papers in order and so nothing can be changed. He must never have known that the property was in your names. Why is it that anything to do with Wills and inheritances and money only brings out the worst in people? I am so glad that I possess nothing, not even a good name. Well, George will certainly have to work now for his bread and butter and that won't be bad for him, either.

Faith and I make a good team in the house and I have been very busy running the farm. I sowed our field over with Timothy grass-seed in addition to oats. The first time that it has been cultivated properly. For the last few years,

THE FIRST YEAR

George does not seem to have had any time or drive to develop the place nor show any real interest in it. We have put in all sorts of vegetables in the two kitchen gardens – turnips, beets, runner-beans, lettuce, radishes as well as about 200 seed potatoes, so we should have plenty and need not buy from the store at Duncans.

The weather has been magnificent all week, bright sunshine and cloudless skies. We all went to Church this morning as usual. Carlo and Charles rode there on their bikes and I drove Faith and Claudia in the small buggy. We took flowers and also wreaths, which we had made at home with crocuses, wild anemones and primroses out of the garden, intertwined with sprays of fir. The children helped us picking the flowers. We all went into the Churchyard and put the wreaths and flowers on Antonia's grave and said a prayer together. Many of her friends had brought flowers too. She is far from being forgotten.

We stayed on for Holy Communion, while Charles went home on his bike and put a steak pie in the oven and fried some potatoes for dinner. He did his share of the cooking very well. School has made him more independent and disciplined. It was the greatest luck that the very first school in Duncans was started only last Autumn and that the headmaster immediately agreed to take him. Antonia had taught him at home and very well, but he probably spent too much time in only feminine company and has been spoiled. Strangely, Charles never mentions her name, not even today, whilst making wreaths. He is completely wrapped up with his life at school. I took him out fishing on Friday evening and we caught six trout, about ¾ of a pound each. They were very good, cooked for breakfast the next day.

It is little Claudia who misses her mother terribly. It is simply heartbreaking when she starts weeping for her, every evening at bedtime. It was so moving in the Churchyard to see how carefully she arranged the flowers for her mother. Luckily she was very tired afterwards and slept in Faith's arms throughout the Service.

I must stop now as it is tea-time. I think that I have answered all your questions. I know that Antonia simply dreaded the operation. It was Carlo who drove her and Faith to the station in the buggy, not me. She said that she wanted to say goodbye to me in her room, alone. So I kissed her there and her last words to me were, "God bless you always, William, and remember to pray to Him for strength and you will come through." Then we came downstairs and I waved to her from the verandah until she was completely out of sight. This is the last I saw of her alive.

She was wearing a red dress.

Ever Yr. affec. Son,

William

"Oakleigh"   12th April, 1909

My dear Son,

After talking matters over with your Father, we have decided to send you a Water-filter, being convinced that some of your aches and pains could be attributed to impure drinking-water from the marshes. We have ordered the two gallon model from Mawson, Swan and Weddell of Newcastle, who are arranging to have it shipped out to you. One of their men, a Mr Perry, is going out to British Columbia to take up a new post with the International

Timber Company at Campbell River. As he is sailing over on the Union Steamship Ferry to Nanaimo, he will accompany the crate as far as Nanaimo station and leave it c/o the Stationmaster. We understand that Nanaimo lies on your railway line. Mr Perry sails from Southampton on May 2nd, so you can enquire towards the end of May if it has arrived.

Instructions on Receiving the Crate

When you receive the crate, carefully remove all straw or packing material from the inside and see that the tap is screwed tightly into position. Place the filter under a tap or pump and allow the water to pass plentifully through it, until the filtered water is quite bright and free from any taste. Then thoroughly clean the filter, inside and out, and place in a convenient and cool position for further use. Once a day, allow the upper portion to run quite empty, so that the air may reach the filtering mediums. Water is best when freshly filtered. The filtering mediums should be renewed about every four to six months and may be obtained from Mawson, price 3/6. (The firm will enclose six new mediums with this order.)

Of course, if you succumb to Rheumatic Fever, nothing is so efficacious as Soda Salix, Salts of the Willow Bark, which takes a fever away in twenty-four hours, which usually last six weeks. Ten grains for a dose.

We decided that we needed a change of air and scene and went to Bath for two weeks to rest and take the waters. Your Father just could not think of going to Buxton again, where we were when we received the news of your sister's departure. Bath, of course, both architecturally and socially outmatches Buxton. Admiral Thornton recommended a Hotel to us and we were very satisfied with both the cooking and service. It lies near the Pulteney Bridge and our rooms had delightful views across the Avon River in the direction of the Weir.

Your Father and I are naturally anxious that Antonia's Will should be proved in all reasonable haste so that you know just where you stand. Alas! we do not trust George and rely entirely on you and Mr Ghirlandi to look after the property in the interests of Charles. Your Father is in continuous contact with Antonia's lawyer in Victoria, who seems to be a most conscientious and serious Scotsman and we are more than relieved that, at the last minute, she had put her affairs in order and in his capable hands. There are so many problems still to be faced.

Earlier this month, I wrote to George at great length about the future of Charles. We feel that, as our only Grandson, he should be sent over to England to school. At this late stage and at the age of sixteen, it will, of course, be very difficult to find a place for him in a good Public School, but we have already made very satisfactory contacts. His holidays can be spent with us. Miss Meare has already written to us. Her first letter, one of condolence, was full of genuine kindness and devout Faith. Her second letter came a week later, containing the proposal that she and her future husband should take over the care of the small girl. It seems that Miss Meare made this promise just before Antonia's operation. She had her confidence and friendship and seems utterly trustworthy. Her future husband, who joined in writing the letter with her, seems to have had the very greatest regard for Antonia and feels that they must fulfil the trust which has been placed in them. Miss

Meare has a most open and sympathetic nature. A woman of sterling qualities, it would seem. George agrees with the proposal and it would be a great relief to us. Your Father is in favour of a legal adoption, but that could be arranged at a later date. We have no doubt that, with God's Help, everything will turn out for the best.

Miss Sutherland and the Staff send their kind regards and your Aunt Bella joins me in affectionate greetings.

Yr. affec.

Mother

P.S. I omitted to mention the Special Precautions to be taken during epidemics or when the water is of doubtful origin. Renew the filtering medium once in two months. Every morning, fill the filter and add a teaspoonful of Solution of Permanganate of Potash (or Condy's Fluid), and allow the water to run plentifully through it until the filtered water is quite bright and free from taste. Instead of the Potash, there may be added to the water a pinch of powdered alum (about two grains to the gallon). As an additional precaution, the water may be boiled and allowed to cool in a covered vessel before being filtered. The filter should be completely emptied every morning and only fresh water used. I trust these instructions are completely clear.

The Fens, Duncans.   16th April, 1909

Dear Aunt Bella,

I hope that this letter will be in time to wish you a very happy return of your birthday. Is the weather behaving nicely and are you able to enjoy longer walks and so get yourself in good trim for your annual Lake District Tour with the Watercolour Society? Do you remember how often Antonia wrote to Father, describing the Spring flowering of the Dogwoods? Now they are just coming into bloom, a truly miraculous sight, but she is no longer here to see them. She did not exaggerate their beauty. I have never seen anything so perfectly luscious. I wish that I were an artist like you and could paint a picture of them as a birthday present for your sitting-room.

Mother will have shown you our letters or told you all about poor Antonia's illness and death. You were always so fond of her that I know the news will have upset you very much. We have now learned from the local doctor and also from the lawyer that she had frequently consulted them both. She had been feeling very ill and been in pain for quite some time, but after receiving Father's cable that I was on my way out to Canada, she decided to postpone a thorough medical over-haul in Victoria until I had arrived. My being here strengthened her in the decision to undergo an operation, hoping that she would be given restored health and strength to carry on. She made such a magnificent show out here, with the charming house and garden and her warm-hearted hospitality, that no one can ever have had even a glimmer of a notion that the marriage was not one of the best. To be honest, she told me that it had been a complete failure from the start. Can one's spirit be eaten up from the inside, like a cancer? Was the illness only the outward sign of a hopelessly destructive situation? What do you think, Aunt? I have to talk to you. Antonia is gone and I cannot keep it all to myself and I do not know what to do. The household is already falling apart. Only Antonia held us together. We trusted her and went to her with all our troubles.

What really worries me is Carlo. Since Antonia went, he has been a completely different fellow, so restless, so discontented and bottled-up, that I have the feeling that he is just longing to get right away from us all. I am scared of talking to him, of offending him so that he walks out on us all, for how can Faith and I ever manage here alone? So I remain cowardly mum. He is away a great deal, carpentering, but always comes home at night and every weekend to help us, which Faith and I appreciate enormously. He works at such a furious pressure that he is always dead tired and, after supper and playing with Claudia, he no longer joins us around the fire for a chat or a read but goes straight off to his shack. I wish I knew what was on his mind and that he would confide in me as he did with Antonia, but it would be wrong for me to force things.

Charles is very happy at school and so that is one relief. Also little Claudia is slowly beginning to accept living with her "Aunt Faith" and her "Doc", and very seldom asks after her mother.

I do not think that I have anything more to add to this tale of woe but I have always been able to talk to you, even as a small boy, and I know that you will find a way to keep this letter and its contents to yourself. It is sometimes useful to be regarded as "eccentric", I think? I had long ago thought that some of your various "ailments" were a cover to enable you to escape Mother's domineering ways and to shut yourself away up in your own rooms, to think your own thoughts in peace and in your own atmosphere of books and painting.

I do so admire how you have always managed to lead your own life. If my remarks and observations seem to be indiscreet or even impertinent, please forgive me.

May this coming year bring you only happiness in all your social and cultural activities and in the company of your numerous friends.

With loving good wishes, dear Aunt,
Ever Yr. affec. Nephew,
William

The Fens.   Sunday 18th April, 1909

My dear Mother,

Thank you very much for your last letter containing so much news and I am especially glad to hear that Father feels so much better, now that the Spring has come. The weather here is quite hot in the day-time but it freezes at night and I am very glad of those warm pyjamas. The post seems to vary so much, from twelve days to over three weeks.

I know that George has written to you and I suppose he has informed you of his future plans, which he keeps from us. I think that he is jealous of us all, I mean of Faith, Carlo, Claudia and myself, because we all had Antonia's love. He had nothing and now he has found out that he does not even own the property, where he played "the Master" for so many years. I pity him, poor fellow! He only

THE FIRST YEAR

gets on well with Charles, who is like him in many ways, although I try not to accept this and am always searching for a glimpse of his mother in him. George and I scarcely ever see each other and hardly speak when we do meet. He is away so much on survey. The job brings him five dollars a week and his keep, luckily for him.

Spring and Summer are the busy times here. For the moment, I know that I must stay on at "The Fens" and help all I can to hold the place together. I feel that you and Father would wish me to do this. No doubt things will shake down in time so please do not worry too much. We must all have patience while we try to adjust ourselves to this totally unexpected situation.

It was a normal Mattins Service at Church today. Mr Leakie preached and even preached well, for him. He is such an uninspiring little man but he means well. I just love to sit in my place in our pew and simply think my own thoughts. Maybe that is not what you think I should be doing in Church, Mother, but it refreshes me to face all the problems of the coming week, as no drink nor tonic could do. Antonia's grave looked so pretty with fresh flowers and wreaths on it. Everybody in the district was fond of her. No one can stand George.

You asked about Faith and Gerald. They plan to get married in the Summer. I do not know how much Antonia told you about her early years here or about Faith. She and Antonia met on the boat coming out from England, all that time ago. Faith was then on her way to take up a post as nurse-governess to a family, the Milnes, in Ottawa. They kept up their voyage friendship, corresponding regularly. Then the Milnes moved to Vancouver and Faith went with them, but when they decided to send their three boys back to schools in England, Antonia asked Faith to come and help her with her coming baby, Claudia. So she came, and has been a tower of strength ever since. Now she has the chance to build up a life for herself, before it is too late. Gerald is a good man, a bit dull but she will be completely safe with him. He also has struggled too long alone and needs a help-mate. This is a pioneer land and life is a lot easier in double harness. It is grand for me to be able to repay a little of the devotion and loyalty that she showed to Antonia by helping Gerald to build their first home. I know that would please her so much. It won't be big – only a large living-room, a smaller dining-room, a bedroom, a kitchen and an out-house, but we will make it homely and it is what they can afford at the moment. They can always add to it later. Carlo will be the architect and builder and I will be the workman's mate.

So I have been busy on their place this week, slashing limbs off fallen trees and otherwise preparing to build a big barn of unpeeled logs, as a start, and to house their stock and all the farming implements which they are purchasing as cheaply as possible, mostly at the weekly auction down in Duncans, where you can get real bargains.

Today we have been splitting fallen trees with powder and making burning log piles. Heavy work but interesting. It is the only way to clear the ground in this country. We will fire the land next Tuesday. It is always a grand sight. The flames seem to go up to a tremendous height. The danger is, of course, causing a bush fire. A man named McCrae started one last week. He let his fires get away from him but they were got out in two days, after having burnt a lot of fences and about a square mile of bush. Luckily it went near no homes.

Charles seems to be enjoying his Easter holidays and has a school-friend, Billy Maitlande, here to stay. We all went fishing together one day and caught two trout which were over a pound and also a foot-long grayling. The boys were very proud, as I let them try with my tackle. I want to be a good influence and I try to think of what Antonia would wish.

I am so glad to hear that Arthur's team did so well. He will have had the proudest moment of his life, like I once had. I miss the sports of England very much. Here, they do not know the meaning of the word, except for sailing and angling, which are not team sports. I keep myself very much to myself, to avoid saying anything wrong or seeming to be critical of my new home. As an outsider, I must feel my way, slowly.

We have been working really hard this Spring. The field that Carlo and I sowed with oats is already showing green. A good crop, I think. We have also put in cabbages, caulies, carrots, spinach, water-melons and marrows. And we have some good raspberry canes, three years old. In the garden near the lake, the soil is very rich. How happy Antonia would be to see it all. I think I am getting better with my hands.

My best love to everybody. It is already nine o'clock and I must rise early tomorrow as it is creamery morning and the cream has to go down to Duncans every Monday and Thursday. Faith and I have doubled our market for it and are very proud of our efforts.

Ever Yr. affec. Son,
William

The Fens.   25th April, 1909

My dear Mother,

Thank you very much for your last letter. I think that I answered all your questions in previous letters. However, now you ask me for my opinion as to Charles' education and future. We all, (that is George, Carlo and I), think that he would do better to continue at school here. His master, Mr Skrimshire, seems a good man and takes a great interest in the boy. He agrees with us that it would be wrong to take him away from his school and his friends and send him so far away to a boarding-school in England, even if he did spend the holidays with his grandparents and would not want for anything that money could buy. The lad is Canadian born and bred, a British Columbian boy. It is hard to explain to you just what I mean, for you have never been away from England in your life. It is wonderful of you to make the offer and I know that you mean it for the best, but he belongs here.

This evening, we three men sat around the fire with him and discussed it all, very openly, in front of him: your offer and what advantages an education at a Public School and a future in England, under his grandparents' guidance, would bring him, but he wants to stay here and we all feel that his decision is the right one The canals of Derbyshire and Cheshire are no waters for a Canadian salmon. I dearly hope, as you do, that one day he will be able and fit to inherit this beautiful property.

George has got a new survey job at 3½ dollars a week and his keep. I hope that he will be able to stick to it. These appointments are very uncertain and he might not keep it for long. His outbursts of bad temper do not help him and actually he has no training for this work.

On Tuesday last, Gerald, Carlo and I fired the slashing, (this means land where all the trees have been felled), on Gerald's property – about five acres in all. It was a grand sight and very successful indeed. We took great care to trench it all round so that it did not spread into the bush. Bush fires are terrible things.

Carlo is off tomorrow to work for Ashby for a week, to cut down trees on a big contract job. Well-paid work. I shall be busy in the kitchen garden. We have a lot of good vegetables. Our hens are also laying well. I have three broodies hatching out and we are setting the other eggs in water-glass for use in the Winter. The calf goes along splendidly and should make a grand cow. She will be kept for milking. Carlo's horse has gone wrong in the hind foot. We have a lot of trouble with her but I hope that she will recover. It would be a big loss for him if she did not, as he rides everywhere to work and his jobs are scattered over a big area.

The oats that we sowed are coming up well and very even, I am glad to say, as it was my very first attempt ever at sowing. Maybe, one day, I will make a good farmer. Nothing that I learned in England has fitted me for the life that I now lead, except to hold a gun, and now I must shoot for the pot and not for any taxidermist.

The animals will be out all the time soon and so I shall have more time for other things. I must get off to bed. Tomorrow, I rise at 5:30 for the creamery day. My best love to anyone who remembers me.

Yr. affec. Son,
William

The Fens.   2nd May, 1909

My dear Mother,

Thank you very much for the last parcel of the local papers. I still find them very interesting. George is still away on survey but he came home yesterday evening and has just left again, taking clean clothes and plenty of good tuck with him. Faith is so good, cooking, washing and mending everything for him with never even a simple "thank you" for all her pains. He always takes everything for granted. I hope he can hold this job down, as the pay is good. He has had a rise.

The man who is the driving force behind this whole new road scheme is a most extraordinary character, a Major MacFarlane, an Irishman and a retired Indian cavalry officer, now living on his property at Mill Bay, some twenty miles from here. He was convinced that a road could be built, as he knew every inch of the country through shooting grouse and pheasant over it. No one believed him and he became the local laughing-stock. So he decided to plot it all alone, secretly, and with only the help of a borrowed map, a compass and an aneroid barometer. It took him three whole Summers to make his plans! Then he got two independent surveyors over from the mainland to confirm his finding as being thoroughly practicable, and then old MacFarlane travelled down to Victoria and worried all the officials there like a bulldog with a juicy bone. He got his plans accepted and the actual work started sometime last year. We tend to ridicule these stubborn old military types from India, but they have guts, determination and no little ability. One has to take one's hat off to them! Of course, the railway people fear competition from a proper road. One day, the islanders will be grateful.

I have been working very hard, clearing off the logs and burning them at Gerald's place. Of course, only in my spare time and to help him, as I am more than busy enough on our own property. The weather has been very hot and dry for some time. The well above the house has now run dry and we have to use the force pump at the creek, which lies about a quarter of a mile from the house. About 500 strokes pump up enough water to last us for two days. Good healthy exercise, walking up there, pumping and walking back, dripping wet, as the pump is very temperamental.

Charles is well and returned happily to school last Monday, without a care in the world, although he is bottom of his form. He is a weekly boarder now. It is better for him, more discipline and it makes life easier for Faith.

You seem to be leading your usual busy social life. Today, we had two men in for tea, (as their wives are away visiting relations on the mainland). A lad from Nosemo, named Gedens and our neighbour, Mr Townsend, who talked us all to death over the assessment of his rates. Round and round the same boring topic until even Faith, patience itself, broke in and changed the conversation over to vegetables. All our kitchen-garden stuff is coming along wonderfully and that gave her the chance to have a rare boast, as we know that Townsend's own crop is not so good and he had lectured us all stiff, for months, on his pet topic of correct vegetable cultivation. Our calf, "Holly", is growing fast and will be a fine cow and a good milker, we hope. But, as you see, our social conversations are not on a very exalted level.

Next week, I am going to put a border around Antonia's grave, probably of local stone. The earth has now settled. How final that sounds! I do miss her most fearfully.

My love to you and to Aunt Bella and kind regards to Miss Sutherland and to all the staff.

Ever Yr. affec. Son,
William

From Mill Bay.   6th May, 1909

Dear Mrs Newton-Lanes,

I wish to thank you for your very kind letter and really it is more than generous of both you and Mr Newton-Lanes to continue sending the monthly remittance through May and June, when it really ought to have been discontinued last month, after Antonia's demise.

As you enquired concerning the operation expenses, do I dare to hope that you intend to settle them? Frankly, I do not know where to find the money.

Dr Jones' fee (the surgeon)	$50
Hospital and nurses	$20
Dr Rolston (Duncans' local doctor)	$5
	$75

I am also enclosing her last dentist's bill for $41, which I found in her writing-desk. By the way, I would just like to mention that Charles' school fees will cost $130 a year, without any extras.

I am very occupied at work on the new road, where I am personally superintending important construction work and so I can only manage to return home late on Saturday afternoons, returning on Sunday evenings. Your property, "The Fens", looks different to me every week at this time of the year and so does Charles. He is now growing at a tremendous rate and promises to be a fine man. Following my advice and instructions, William is taking him in hand with a view to developing his muscles generally, and he is training Charles for the School Sports' Day next month, which event I hope to attend, if my onerous duties permit.

There is one urgent matter which I am obliged to bring to your notice. I have taken legal advice and my lawyer, Mr Crease, tells me that I must obtain your answer to this question, purely as a matter of form, before Antonia's Will can be proved, and that is:-

Is there any legacy that you know of that must legally revert to me or to her heirs?

One does so hate the idea of appealing to the law at these times, but I wish to have all matters settled correctly. At Antonia's death, I seized the opportunity and immediately drew up my own Will, so arranging matters that both William and Carlo will always be sure of "The Fens" as their home, not only during my lifetime but also until the time Charles reaches the age of twenty-five and inherits the property. I think that you will appreciate my generous arrangements.

We are having an extraordinarily dry Spring. At home, the men have had to begin using the force pump a month earlier than usual.

In your letter, you mentioned that you were intending to go away. I trust that the change of air and scene will do you good and lead to renewed health and vigour.

I await your reply and remain, believe me,
Yours sincerely,
George Carfax

The Fens.   Sunday 9th May, 1909

My dear Mother,

Thank you for your last welcomed letter. I am sorry if
I have given you the wrong impression. You are not to
worry. George is quite a good father to Charles but he
leaves Claudia entirely to Faith. It is really very strange but
he ignores her completely. And she him. He has been home
since last night but returns to a new stretch of the road near
Cobble Hill this afternoon. He tells me that he has written
to you about his future plans. He has discussed nothing
with us, which is typical of the man.

It has been very difficult to get jobs out here since last
year's slump. The Yankees have stopped investing and the
price of copper has dropped and several mining-towns have
folded up. The boom is over, let us hope only temporarily.
It has been very hard for many families and there have been
some real tragedies. Lucky for us that we farm and will
never starve.

Last week I was busy making log piles and burning
them, so as to clear more of our land for pasture next year.
Very hard physical work, as the logs are about thirty feet
long and have to be rolled together with cart hooks, blocks
and wedges. I have lost well over a stone in weight since I
came out and am now quite spare, but my health is pretty
good, apart from rheumatics. Have you or Aunt Bella got a
simple home remedy for this plague?

I hope that Arthur enjoyed his first international match in Cardiff. I see that England won easily enough, but it is good that Wales can raise such a fine team. I was a member of the touring teams that started the game in Wales some years ago. I shall never be there again, never hear the cheers at the close of a winning game. That part of my life is all over and I must stop hankering after the past.

We had some rain today, which was badly needed as everything was getting burnt by the heat. Farming here is one long grind. Our cows are doing well and giving more milk since they were turned out at night into the pasture. Ten more chickens arrived during a storm on Friday. Faith and I thawed them out and dried them on a blanket in front of the kitchen stove and now they are doing splendidly. Our kitchen garden thrives and will be all the better for today's rain, for which we had prayed most earnestly in Church today – and *instantly* received. Not having taken our umbrellas, we all arrived home simply drenched through!

The creamery days are now Monday, Wednesday and Friday as the cream will not keep long in this heat and it is over an hour's drive down to Duncans. I wonder and worry how we shall get on when Faith gets married. I expect that I shall have to mend the clothes and socks. I am already hair-cutter-in-chief and keep all their heads smart. I have grown a nice, even beard which saves me so much shaving-time in the mornings. Strangely enough, it is a foxy red!

Last auction day, I acquired a beautiful wooden mould for the butter – a fat cow with a huge bell round her neck. I think that it must have come originally from a Swiss farm-house. Where is that family now? Whilst working, I have so much time to think, mostly about fate. Antonia firmly believed that our lives are pre-destined, that it is all in our stars, but I am certain now that there are moments in our lives when we come to a sort of cross-road and are presented with a choice. She need never have married George and gone out with him to Canada. She could have caught her train and left him in the Waiting-room at Crewe station. I should have had the courage to come to Father, instead of letting myself be blackmailed. We both acted as we did. She suffered and is now dead. I wonder what further price I may have to pay. Oh! if only she had lived, we could have helped each other so much. No more for now. My best love to you all,

 Yr. affec. Son,
 William

The Fens.   Sunday 16th May, 1909

My dear Mother,

Thank you for your interesting letter about the Rector's last sermon. I received it yesterday and also the *Athletic News*. It is very good of you to arrange to send the Water-filter out with Mr Perry. You wrote that he is coming over from Vancouver on the Union Steamship Ferry to Nanaimo and I can easily arrange for someone to bring it down from there. A good thing that you gave me such full working instructions in your letter as we are all dependent on our own poor brains and hands out here. I had a good laugh over your instructions to get the water "from a tap or pump". Here, every drop must be drawn from the well that lies below the house and which is fed by an underground stream, when it is not dried out.

We have, however, had steady rain for three days this week, which we needed badly, as the crops and vegetables were getting dried up and also the wild flowers. The bush is a mass of brilliant, rippling blue "Kamass", which is rather like the English Bluebell. This flower has a fleshy, deep-rooted bulb, which is an important food for the Indians, who cook it as a vegetable. Then there are two flowers that I have never seen before – the "Trillium Lily", with its three pure-white petals, and the purple "Calypso Orchid". They are flowering now in the marshes. The "Wild Rose" is also a joy and reminds me of the hedges at home. This was Antonia's favourite month of the whole year. Today the sun is shining again and she would surely have been out in her boat, sketching in the marshes.

Carlo has been employed all the past week making fly-screens for the windows at Hadmen's place. They had such a mosquito plague last year and, now that they have a new baby, they want to be protected. George is home for the weekend. He seems to be getting on all right with his boss, which is a mercy. Carlo and Faith are bothered by their rheumatism but mine is better. I don't know why. Charles seems very well and in good form. Nothing seems to bother him very much and I sometimes wonder how much depth there is to him. Antonia's influence has gone, George spoils him completely and Faith and I pick up the pieces, as best as we can. My role has become the heavy-handed Uncle. Not one that I like, but I do try to interest him in games and sport and, as his School Sports' Day comes along soon, I have worked out a training schedule for him at the weekends. Perhaps success in sport will spur him on. Claudia, on the other hand, is a constant joy. She seems, at last, to accept that her mother will never come back and seldom cries for her. She loves "playing the piano" with Faith – with one finger and thumb.

Gerald has now got all the plans for the new house, which Carlo has designed. Tomorrow we shall get the lumber up from Duncans and set about making it for them right away.

A friend of mine, Jack Pooley, has gone up north to Prince Rupert to work for a Swedish laundry-man. He does not like it much but the pay is very good. Pooley is a certified engineer and so that got him the contract. Twenty dollars a week, but he has to keep and board himself and is tied down for a year to do the job. But beggars can't be choosers.

This place is only work, eat and sleep, day after day, principally work. They say that it is good for one, but is that all there is to life? I am still trying to find the answer.

My best love to everyone who remembers me. I must go to bed as tomorrow starts at 5:30 and ends at seven in the evening. A long day.

Ever Yr. affec. Son,
William

"Oakleigh"   28th May, 1909

My dear Son,

At last I can write again. I had to ask Miss Sutherland to pack up and post your birthday parcel, containing four warm, striped flannel shirts, which I hope will help your rheumatic condition. I must apologise for my slovenly script. Nearly a month ago, I slipped on Miss Pendlebury's garden steps whilst admiring her Forsythias and sprained my right wrist, nothing serious, but Dr Martin prescribed cold-water poultices and insisted that I rest my hand in a sling for ten days.

I do not know what to advise you about your rheumatism. Mr Sykes has had it for years, but it is now so bad that we have had to engage a young lad to help him with the digging and the heavy work in the garden, as he simply cannot manage on his own anymore. The new boy has already made a good job of putting fresh gravel on the drive and paths. It is no use to send you Dr Sloan's Liniment because the bottles would only break in the post and the only cure that I know of is to visit a Spa. For you now quite out of the question.

We had bought a new, slow-combustion stove for the kitchen and also a new rustless boiler for the wash-house and they are now installed. We had to postpone all the previous arrangements, as we were far too upset by Antonia's sudden death to think of having workmen in the house. The three new grates in the drawing-room, library and my sitting-room are now all fitted. Bondy's Marble Masons have repaired and re-set the mantelpieces very well.

Early this month and while all this work was going on, we travelled by rail to London, staying overnight at my Sister's, your Aunt Agatha's, new and most comfortable home in the Cromwell Road, Kensington, and so on to Southampton, where we took the boat over to Jersey, to stay in Mrs LeBrun's Hotel. The long journey cost nearly £10 but it was more than worth the expenditure as our stay was pleasant, the climate balmy after the northern Winter, and so we both recovered our spirits in the congenial surroundings. The service was excellent and such consideration was shown to us. The other guests were most agreeable and your

Father made several long walks with a Colonel Fitzgerald, recently bereaved. I wore my new alpaca dress, which Miss Robinson had made for me, for the journey, and my wardrobe was much admired. I had given considerable thought and time to it because, even in bereavement, one need not appear slovenly.

We have a new Station-master, replacing old Chapman, who has retired. Lewis, the blacksmith, died suddenly of heart failure last week.

Just before we came away, we had a bad scare. A kitchen window was broken in the night and two more windows on the following night. After the third occasion, at nine o'clock, when the scullery window was smashed to smithereens, a policeman was sent to watch, all day and night, posted in the thick shubbery at the back of the house. It was Maude's mother! She had broken the windows because we had docked Maude's pay, for deliberate care-lessness whilst washing-up the Crown Derby tea-service. Of course Maude has been dismissed and we informed the police that that was the end of the matter, as far as we were concerned. The broken panes have already been replaced. A new house-maid, Nellie, came today, with excellent ref-erences from our Bank Manager. She has been very well trained and is a most pleasant girl, and quiet, which Maude never learnt to be.

Just before we left home for Jersey and the carriage was actually at the door, Mr and Mrs Alfred Diggles called, being on their Wedding Tour. Alas! we could not stop to invite them in but they should have written to inform us of their intention to call.

This letter is only full of household woes but I am happy to say that we are all in good health though still suffering deeply from our great loss. It has aged your Father considerably, coming so close on top of all his anxieties on your behalf, earlier in the year. 1909 is not proving to be a lucky year, except for our dear Arthur, who moves up to Scotland, to Aberdeen, in July to take up his new position. Alas! he will be so far away from us.

I have had to write a very sharp letter to George about the payments of all of Antonia's bills. Of course your Father generously insists on settling everything, but I never liked or trusted George and find it very hard to write to him. An even moderately polite letter taxes my sense of charity. I am convinced that he pocketed the money which Antonia must have given him to settle her dentist's bill from last year. Your Father simply refuses to write to him himself and has left this unpleasant task to me. I cannot visualise either George's future or yours without our regular financial help, but we are very pleased to hear how you have knuckled-down to the hard life out in British Columbia and that you are learning to farm properly and are proving yourself, with God's help.

Please remember me kindly to all at "The Fens".
Ever Yr. affec.
Mother

"Oakleigh"   1st June, 1909

Dear Mr Carfax,

Thank you for your letter of the 6th May with the detailed accounts for Antonia's operation and the exact cost of it, inclusive. Also the bill of having her teeth put right. We note, however, that this bill was from 1908, and we have deemed it only fit and polite to write a covering letter of apology to the dentist concerned, Mr Garesche of Victoria.

I enclose a money order for £10 for the month of June:- that is, £4 for William's board, £4 as before, (Antonia's remittance) and £2 from my sister for the two children.

To pay all the bills that you enclosed, I have sent the money, in dollars, directly to the doctors and dentist concerned, as well as to the hospital in Victoria. We will also pay all the expenses of the funeral, if you will tell us what they were, as well as enclosing *detailed* bills from the undertaker. We can then settle his account personally.

With regard to your question as to any legacy coming to Antonia, the only one is the £3,000 left her by my father, less the £1,500 we lent to Antonia on the security of it, to start you off in your life at "The Fens", as you may well remember. This leaves the sum of £1,500 but, by my father's Will, I have a life interest in this legacy and I am pleased to report that I am in excellent health.

I trust this answers your questions and that the lawyer in Victoria can now have the Will proved. Incidentally, Antonia sent her father a copy of her last Will, which she made on the 25th February inst. and so we were fully aware of her intentions, for we had discussed them in our letters to her and approved them. Although the property is in our names, we naturally regarded the furniture and all moveable goods and chattels to be your joint possessions. You seem to have forgotten that her father is a lawyer.

Our best wishes to all at "The Fens".

Yours sincerely,

Agnes Newton-Lanes

(Across the top was written: – This is a copy of my letter to George, to be kept with all the receipted bills, when received, in case he should claim these sums again.)

The Fens, Duncans Station.   20th June, 1909

My dear Mother,

Thank you very much for your kind birthday letter and also for the gift of the shirts. It was very good of you to think of me.

The weather here is very hot. George has applied for a government appointment in the Survey Office. I will let you know what arrangements we come to when he hears the result. If he is successful, that means that he must move to Victoria, so what will happen to the house then? However, I do hope that he gets this job. The pay is seventy-five dollars a month, to start with. He seems to think that he has good friends who will push him. I must stop now as more water needs pumping. Faith is calling for me.

2nd July

This letter does not seem to get any further as we have so much to do. We have started on Faith's house, working from six to eight o'clock each evening. I have so many chores on our place that I can only help occasionally but I am over there every hour that I can spare. Her house is the most important item on our agenda at the moment. It will be a very nice home, indeed, I think. Faith is so excited about it, her very first home of her own and she is over thirty, just between the two of us.

I am clearing an acre for potatoes next Spring, logging, blowing out stumps and burning. You put a stick of dynamite in the tree-stump and then let it burn right out. Quite a tricky job. I have borrowed a pair of oxen from Aitkin to plough the land and they manure it as they work! This area is too heavy for horses. Soon we shall be busy with the hay, scything where the mower cannot go. I have learned to scythe and find it to be a healthy exercise for loosening my stiff back and shoulder muscles. I thought that it must be a difficult job, until I saw an old man of over eighty swinging away at it. It is all a knack. We have a good crop and hope the weather will keep fine and dry. Our potatoes are doing nicely too. The soil here seems good, when you get enough cleared to cultivate it.

"Oakleigh" must be looking very smart with the new boiler and stove and grates installed. I am glad that you found a young boy to help in the garden. I could do with one here. Sykes must feel really old now, wracked with rheumatism, like I am. Who would ever have thought of that happening to me?

One of our neighbours, Kahmer, has Diabetes, poor fellow, and is having to sell up his place and go back home for treatment. He had just got going so well and had worked terrifically hard, as he came out with nothing, and could only afford a few acres of rather unfavourable land. He is of North German stock, from Stettin, I believe, and a really good chap. It seems very hard lines on him and he was just planning to get married to a local girl. We have all handed the hat round to collect for his return fare by rail and ship back to Europe. He may not make it.

I must stop now. More chores! My letters are only full of work and local news of people whom you will never meet — and would certainly also never meet if you came across them at home.

Sometimes it seems so senseless to write every week. The jobs I do and the folk I meet are so utterly unrelated to life at "Oakleigh".

My best love to yourself. Kind regards to Miss

Sutherland and the staff. I am so glad that the new house-maid is a pearl.

Yr. affec. Son,
William

The Fens, Duncans Station.   5th Sept., 1909

My dear Mother,

Thank you very much for your kind letters and for all the papers and magazines which come so regularly. I recognise Miss Sutherland's handwriting on many parcels so please thank her from me. We all hand our papers around when we have read them, and I even find myself glancing into *The Needlewoman*, for want of some reading matter. Faith's sister sends it out to her from Somerset. Her family lives near Frome. A pretty place, it seems.

I should have written before but I have had a bad hand. I managed to get a bit of rusted tin into it and it was rather nasty for some days. We managed to get it out with Faith's pinking scissors, of all strange surgical instruments. I was strengthened for the "operation" by a very generous tot of ship's rum from Carlo. He received it recently, a whole bottle, in lieu of a cash payment for a job that he had done down on a boat at Maple Bay harbour!

We got our hay in, after some trouble. Rather a disappointingly small crop but our oats are good. A Scotsman, McRae, helped me with the hay and our neighbour, Aitkin, hauled for us with his heavy oxen team. Everyone helps the other fellow out here. We could none of us manage otherwise, but there is a strict line drawn between jobs for which you are engaged and paid, and mere neighbourly helping-out.

We are now very busy with Faith's house. We still have the lining of the walls to do. She is to be married on Tuesday 14th Sept. in Victoria where both have many friends. I am to be the Best Man. Carlo has given them a Morris chair and I have given them two basket chairs for their porch. We bid for them at a recent sale and they are all as good as new. I managed to save about $50, up to the present, out of my work this summer. The Winter is a very slack time for work and everyone stays at home, generally clearing their own land and doing repairs. I hear that it can be very cold and muddy before the first snows come.

George is still on the road. His application for that Government job was turned down and he apparently has no plans for the Winter. Charles went back to school yesterday. A relief to me and to Faith, as it is so difficult to be working and also keeping an eye on a sixteen-year-old who is very keen to avoid any work or orders, and I refuse to let him get out of hand. Carlo and I are planning what to do when Faith leaves us. I expect we shall do our own mending and darning in the evenings, when work is over. We cannot afford to engage a woman to do it and anyway I doubt if we could find one. The Indians do not like their women working for bachelors.

Faith and Gerald cannot afford a honeymoon and so will be returning to their new home directly after the wedding celebrations. Claudia will then be over in their house all day and one of us will always collect her for tea each evening, enjoy some play-time with her and see her washed and off to bed. She sleeps very soundly in the room next to mine and has now graduated to a cup of morning tea. Until George knows what he is doing, it seems to be the only practical solution. I have suggested to George that he give Faith half of the remittance which you are still sending, that is £2, which was Antonia's share of the money, as she is now caring for Claudia for the greater part of the day, and also £1 of Aunt Bella's gift for Claudia – £3 in all. George was pocketing it *all* and I shamed him into agreeing. I hope that you find this to be right and fair? Without her help, we would be lost and it is also a great responsibility for her. They need every cent, too. It seems that she did know the full truth about Antonia's health, long before the operation, and that she promised Antonia, even long before she went into the hospital, that she would always care for Claudia.

Carlo and I are alone today. He sends his kind regards. We have already lit the fire as the evening is chilly. We are burning some Douglas Fir and are making scones for tea, as a surprise for Faith, when she returns from taking Claudia and two other small children to the sea for the day in the buggy. They are not back yet, but two of the most hospitable smells in the world will greet them as they come in. She is so good to the child, really loves her dearly and they are now devoted to each other. Claudia will be one of her two bridesmaids. I hear the sound of the buggy wheels, so they are back safely.

My best love to you and kind regards to everyone at home.

Yr. affec. Son,
William

WILLIAM'S STORY

The Fens, Duncans Station.   22nd Nov., 1909

My dear Mother,

You seem to have had so many visitors this past Summer and Autumn and numerous social events. It is a life which I have almost forgotten, but we have been busy, too, and that is my apology for not writing since sometime in September. We managed to finish the house for Gerald and Faith on time and now they have been in residence nearly two months and are simply thrilled with everything and can find no fault with our workmanship, which does make us very proud men.

I spent one whole day with them, helping with the furniture, which had come out from England. Their two families gave them a complete outfit for the living-room and bedroom as a joint wedding gift from them all. Everyone joined in and I think that this was a simply splendid effort. Of course, we do our own "removals" here. You would have been amazed to see us trifling with wash-stands, chests-of-drawers, wardrobes and handy little pieces of that size and weight. Really, I think that the house is very nice and a great credit to Carlo, who designed it for them and who was also the chief carpenter. I, of course, was only the mate, but I did lay all the flooring and quite alone, too. We had no accident of any kind whilst we were building it. Rather a rare thing in these parts but, as we are both very tall and heavy men, we had taken great care over the scaffolding.

The wedding took place in Victoria and after the reception, I went straight from there by boat to Seattle for a few days' holiday. It is a lovely sail, passing uninhabited islands and the great range of the snow-covered Olympic

Mountains. The change of air did me good, although the seas were pretty choppy. In Seattle, I did three theatres and two music halls.

Seattle is a large and up-to-date American city, boasting five Motion Picture Houses, but those do not interest me. However, I was most fortunate to be able to hear both "Carmen" and "Aida", performed by the International Opera Company at the Moore Theatre. I went along and sat in the gallery and shut my eyes most of the time, imagining myself to be with Aunt Agatha in her box at the Royal Opera House, Covent Garden! That was always the highlight of my annual visit to her. As I went on this trip to Seattle with two other fellows, I also had to fit in with their tastes, which are not mine. So, together, we saw the Russell-Drew Stock Company perform "Queen of the White Slaves" at the Seattle Theatre and also two evenings of vaudeville at the Orpheum and the Majestic, which we were informed gave the best performance of the five vaudeville theatres in Seattle. I dread to think what the other three were like! So that was not very lofty entertainment but I enjoyed myself in a quiet way and brought back a lot of new jokes with which to liven up the Cowichan Valley. Carlo will take his holiday later on. One of us must stay here to look after the livestock.

Charles is well and he may even write to you one day, he says. I was astonished to learn that he has never written to his grandparents in his life – nor you to him. His only interest is shooting and today he shot some Blue and Willow Grouse. A welcomed change for our pot! I still get breakfast for us all and the other meals we manage between us, as we both can cook better than the average female. Carlo even produces a few Italian specialities to ring the change for our evening meal. Faith still does Charles' mending (simply appalling). So good of her. We each do our own.

A friend, who has a good job with a mining company, has bought ten acres near Quamichan Lake and intends to build in the Spring. He has contracted Carlo to clear the bush and fell the trees and Carlo has asked me to help him. We have to finish by March. We can only work on fine days but can take our time over it, so it will be a nice Winter job and good money. I am trying so hard to save for a place of my own. I am getting sick of slaving away on other people's land. Have you got over your "tiredness" and are you fit again? We have all had streaming colds, otherwise we are well, healthy and hard. There is no time to be otherwise.

Our social life is not like yours but we did have two very pretty weddings in our Church, to both of which I was invited. One local girl, Nellie Robertson, married a Mr Walker from Texas, whom she had met on the Seattle boat last year. A real romance! Another local girl, Miss Kingston, married that nice young fellow who helped me with the hay this Summer, McRae.

Dear Antonia's grave looks very nice. We often go there, after Church, just to stand and remember and to say a prayer. Not that she is ever very far away from our thoughts, by day or night. I will never forget her, her love for me and all her encouragement.

Very best love to you all. I will write again when I have time or any news.

Yr. affec. Son,
William

The Fens.   9th Dec., 1909

My dear Mother,

This is my Christmas letter to you. I wish you a
very happy one and "all the Compliments of the Season",
as the printed cards say. This is my first Christmas
ever away from home. We are joining forces with Gerald
and Faith and should be a merry party. Carlo and I have
been busy making Christmas puddings and mince-pies
from Faith's recipes, and which will be our contribution to
the Festive Dinner. Claudia will make paper-chains and
decorate the tree, she announces. Antonia always did that,
it seems.

My last letter will have been delayed as we have been
cut off from Victoria by wash-outs on the line, very deep
floods indeed and the heaviest rainfall in these parts for
twenty-eight years. However, I have been kept occupied
sawing cordwood for the kitchen stove. We had a tiring day
hauling it in and also getting in bark for the sitting-room
fire, which makes a grand blaze in the evenings, when we
sit around the fire, reading and talking and playing
with Claudia. Quite like the old times when Antonia was
with us. Yesterday evening, I spent the time darning socks,
sixteen pairs. Now I understand why Miss Sutherland
always finds it trying to her eyes. She should *never* do it by
lamplight.

It has been snowing deeply for two days and so
stopped all outside work, including our job over at
Quamichan. Carlo shot a deer, which grieved me, but it will
make a change in our menu. Today we will have some of it
stewed with garden vegetables. Butter-making is one of
today's jobs. I get a good sale for it – my "Swiss Butter", as

it is called, for I stamp it with that old wooden Swiss mould. I think I told you about it.

George has not been home for a month. There are no trains and we are completely cut off. He has been moved to the middle section of the road and is having a shack built for him to live in, as he will be working there most of the Winter, which is grand for him and a great relief for us. A Winter snowed-in with George does not bear contemplating.

We had our General Election the other day. Our member, a Conservative, got in by a large majority. The Opposition consists now of three Liberals and two Socialists, the other forty-eight seats are all held by the Conservatives. We have given the Old Country a good lead. Let us hope that she follows us!

Yesterday, old Mr Robinson called in unexpectedly at lunchtime and stayed on for tea. He got Pot Luck. By the way, he told me that some think that our expression, "Pot Luck", may come from the Indians' "Potlach". Some people think that maybe ten thousand years ago, the Indians crossed over the ice from Siberia, where now the Bering Strait flows. But one old Indian chief once told me that they have always been here and somehow I believe him. He said that their ancestors were dropped by an eagle on a desolate mountain-top, near here. It is the same one that I once climbed shortly after arriving here. No wonder that it seemed to be haunted, for it is sacred.

Old Robinson has recently been bereaved, poor fellow. They were a devoted couple and really old pioneers out here in the west. He talked all day to me, keeping me highly entertained with all his reminiscences, the folk-lore and the local gossip, while I was busy mangling and ironing. He says that I have missed my true vocation. I ought to have been a General Servant, "strong and willing", as the adverts always put it. "Can also manage livestock", would be the right description for me, he said. You could have saved a packet on my expensive education, all those years.

We have had tremendous rains and floods and a railway bridge, just north of this place, was washed away — a bridge over 300 feet long. It will be an awkward job to replace it and meanwhile we are completely cut off. Luckily we have a good store of kerosene and wood and our own produce.

I should very much like to join in any presents that you may be giving to Aunt Bella, Miss Sutherland, Sykes and the maids. I will send you my share in cash, if you will let me know how much it is. There is simply nothing suitable to buy out here. Nothing unsuitable, either.

My first year out here is drawing to a close. It was not as any of us could ever have foreseen.

I wonder what the year 1910 will hold in store for me? I think that I have, at least, found my feet out here, but that is all that I can say.

Please think of me sometimes and try to believe in me. I am doing my best.

Fondest Christmas Greetings to one and all.

Ever Yr. affec. Son,

William

THE SECOND YEAR
1910

The Fens, Duncans Station.   10th Jan., 1910

My dear Mother,

Thank you very much for your most kind Christmas wishes and for all the presents. It was very good of you and everything that you sent is more than welcomed, especially the half-dozen pairs of socks and the Jaeger underwear. The riding-breeches are a perfect fit and such good quality. They will last me a lifetime out here.

We enjoyed ourselves very much over at the Carruthers' home. Faith had cooked an excellent goose dinner with all the trimmings and we stayed till late in the evening, playing games and singing all the old carols. In the morning, we had been to Church and it was simply packed. The women had decorated it beautifully with holly and fir branches. We sang all my favourite hymns, too. We seven sat together and so filled two pews, one behind the other, which is much nicer than having to share with another family. In our Church, you can sit anywhere you like and only custom reserves you your regular place, not a pew-fee and social rank, as at home.

We had arrived early so as to have time to put fresh fir-branches on Antonia's grave and to say a prayer for her.

George was home for three days and so we were united again and all were determined to make it a happy Christmas and to let bygones be bygones. He was much more cheerful, likes his job on the new road and seems to think that it will take another year to complete. He never comments on the work we do on this place and actually treats the home simply as a hotel, run for his comfort. He is a strange man. We are too proud to fish for compliments – not that we would ever get any. We are both really, in our hearts, still working for Antonia. That is what keeps us going.

Carlo, George and Charles have gone off to skate, but I have stayed at home to play with Claudia and to write to you. The men organised several good games of Ice Hockey over the past weeks. I played one match but felt too cheap to play again. I was so stiff and slow, had completely lost my eye and bungled far too many passes. I played really damned badly and I know that everyone was expecting great things of me, knowing something of what I had achieved in sport in the Old Country. Now I have lost all my interest in games. I suppose I was still dreaming that I might one day return and play in an international game again. Now you might as well put up old Sykes for my place in any team. What a bad joke! Please stop sending me the *Athletic News*. I want to cut off all sporting contacts with home, which in any case only existed in my rather poor fantasy. I *must* make decisions about my own future. This year, I must make a completely new and independent start.

Many Christmas parcels have not arrived for the folk here. The trains over the plains and across the Rockies are very delayed, owing to the tremendously deep snow drifts. I hate the snow. It looks very nice on a Christmas card from home, but not here. I am glad that you posted your parcel so early.

This is our Wash-day, but our old Indian granny has not come to help. The snow is too deep around here. I am glad, as I have only just finished all the ironing and mending from the last time. I am still fearfully slow at everything, but thorough.

The horses have just come up from having a run in the large field and I must put them into the stable. Anyway, I have no more news about anything that could possibly be of any interest to you. So, goodbye.

Yr. affec. Son,
William

The Fens, Duncans Station.   10th Jan., 1910

My dear Aunt Bella,

Thank you very much for your Christmas greetings and for the grand parcel. The cardigan is a perfect fit and I like the autumn-leaf colour very much. It matches my tweed jacket perfectly. The two pipes are splendid. I am smoking one now, as I write, the Cherrywood, and enjoying it very much indeed. We all smoke "T and B" plug on this side of the earth as it is cheap, lasts a long time and is fairly good.

I have had influenza since last week and still feel very seedy and weak. I could not lay up at all as there is so much for one man to do on this place. I just had to be content with going straight off to bed the moment my jobs were all done. A year ago, this place was being run by three men, (George was seldom away then) and two women, with an Indian woman coming in daily to help. Now I am virtually alone here, the only person in this large house. I have shut up all the upstairs rooms, except Charles' and George's, and put dust-sheets over all the furniture. Claudia has the little downstairs room next to mine.

Faith and Gerald are very happy in their new home,

pleased with their married life, and in confidence, Faith is in "the family way". It is a joy to see them. Gerald is so good to Claudia, too. She practically lives there now, only coming home for our weekends, which she and I and Carlo share together. Carlo has built a room for her at Faith's place, off the living-room and with both east and south windows to catch all the sun. It was Gerald's suggestion and he paid for it.

He is such a good chap, very sound. Faith and I are teaching Claudia to read. As she could already read musical notes, (simply picked up from sitting beside her mother on the piano stool), she is forging ahead. You asked me for Faith's address. The house is called "Frome", after the place in Somerset from where her family came, so the address is "Frome", Duncans Station. That is enough.

The house is now entirely furnished and exceedingly comfortable and warm. The entire cost of the building – lumber, labour, chimney, (the most expensive item out here), and everything else came to a little over 900 dollars, a very cheap house indeed, even for this country. She will be sending you a photo of it, as soon as the photographer comes up from Victoria in the Spring, when he makes his annual round.

Carlo has given up the job at Quamichan, clearing the bush for a fellow. At first the weather was too bad to work and then I was to have helped him, but now, with this illness, I can only just get through my jobs here and would not have been fit enough to help him on an all-day outside job. It is very good of him to make this financial sacrifice but he sees that he is really needed here and he is just taking any odd local job to fill in until I am fit again, and can pull my weight.

As usual, I am going to unburden myself to you. I must talk to someone or bust. This situation just cannot go on. Carlo and I are working for a ghost. I mean Antonia, as we promised her to keep the place going as she would have liked it to be. We had talked over so many plans with her for the future, the improvements, the stock, the gardens. George has simply no interest in the place at all – quite understandable as it is not his property. Of course his job keeps him far away from home but I think he wants it to be like that.

Carlo is a completely changed man since Antonia went and now, in the evenings, he often talks of returning to see his parents in Italy. That would be the final blow. When he first told me, I was simply knocked flat and felt indescribably low. I think that is why I caught this attack of bronchial Flu. I could never manage a place as big as this on my own. So, I must think about my own future and try to get a few acres of my own. For this, I need some capital – not much by English standards. I cannot approach Father as he has cut himself off from me, and is behind a wall of silence. It is Mother who sends the monthly remittances. I think that I have proved that I can knuckle-down to a job, haven't I? I *have* to stay out in Canada and make this land my home. I have no alternative. Did I ever tell you that, since Antonia died, our Barn Swallows have never returned to nest? They came first, the very first Spring after the house was built in 1890 and returned, year after year, to patch up their rough mud nests in the projections under the eaves. Out here, when an Owl calls to you or when your own Swallows desert you, that portends death. I never knew that before. It is true.

My best love to you, dear Aunt Bella, and please do your best to help me.

Ever Yr. affec. Nephew,
William

The Fens, Duncans Sta. 17th Apr., 1910

My dear Mother,

Thank you very much for your kind letters and for your offer to pay for the doctor but that is not necessary for I doctored myself with Quinine and so managed without one.

We have since then been busy on the inside lining etc. of McRae's house. He was the man who helped me to get in the hay last Summer and is a fine fellow, two inches taller than I am and very powerful. One Saturday, before we had finished McRae's house, George told me that he was going to hire Japs to clear some land for him that he has bought. That meant my giving up my job at McRae's in order to stay and supervise them, so we compromised by my taking on George's clearing as a paid job, so as not to be out of work or lose money. When I told McRae, he barked, "What does George want with Japs when he can get any number of white men?" The answer is that they are cheap labour. Of course it means that I do the dangerous work, boring holes under the stumps, putting in the powder and fuses, lighting the fuses, and then run and watch the tree come down from a safe distance (dangerous but fascinating work). The Japs will only do the clearing, the "coolie work" that I usually do, too. The stumps, roots etc. are then collected in large piles and burnt. Some of the piles are so big that they take over a week to burn.

The field is finished now, ploughed, a crop of oats put in and harrowed. I hope to finish my other clearing, about two acres, in a week's time. It will have taken three boxes of powder, about 150 lbs. altogether. The work done is simply tremendous. Later on, McRae may have some fencing for me to do but that is not settled yet.

Carlo and I carted some ten tons of manure in one day last week and spread it on the two fields. So we are hoping for a heavier crop this year.

Please excuse all this talk about myself and of my work but nothing else ever happens.

Charles was confirmed today. We all went and stayed to Holy Communion afterwards, his very first.

Again many, many thanks for all your letters and I nearly forgot your birthday! Very many happy returns of the day to you! My best love to everybody.

Yr. affec. Son,
William

The Fens.   20th June, 1910

My dear Mother,

Thank you so much for your kind birthday wishes. It was very good of you to send me such perfect presents. The new razor is grand, the house-shoes just the right size and very warm and the sou'wester will be invaluable. I just do not know how you can guess what I need out here! You really seem to possess the gift of second sight!

Carlo and I finished the clearing in good time to

plough and get potatoes in, and they are coming along nicely. I go over them every week with the horse cultivator and George says that I am to have half the profits. Since having a royal bust-up with George, he now handles me more like a partner in the concern and less like Jap or Indian labour (unpaid, at that). He even admitted that my work is improving the value of the property. He seems now to be looking ahead towards his future inheritance, others having told him what the purchase price would be, today.

McRae and I had a job together, cutting and putting up telephone posts for the Telephone Co. Rather a heavy and dangerous job, if the post slips just when you are raising it. We had a stretch of about two miles to do. A well-paid job. McRae recommended me, which was most kind of him. He is a good chap and knew that I need the money badly. Then I had a day with Townsend, removing the floor of his chicken-house and putting fresh battens. A fine, smelly job! I also had three days of work making a chicken-run for Gerald, ninety feet by ten feet. His chicks are doing well. Since finishing that, I have been building another chicken-house with Carlo for McRae. We finished that last week. It is 150 feet long by ten feet wide. So I have earned quite a bit this Summer towards my own place.

Now I am planning to build a studio for Carlo at his shack, complete with sky-light. Did I ever tell you that he is actually a professional painter and studied in an Art School in Florence? I am working on this idea of a studio in the hope of persuading him to stay on here and take up his old profession again. Some folk here were going back to the Old Country and wanted pictures of their places to take with them as a keepsake. Carlo painted lovely water-colours of their houses and barns and both families were really delighted. He could do this sort of thing as a start and then gradually get established and make some money at it. Perhaps even collect enough pictures of life in the Cowichan Valley to have a show, down in Victoria, where there is the big money.

It was he who taught Antonia to paint water-colours and he says that she was a really gifted painter, better than he. She was so many-sided, so very talented. All wasted out here.

26th June.

I had not time to finish this letter as I have been in the throes of hay-making. I had all the arranging to make for the cutting and hauling. Also I did all the scything between the stumps and around the fences, where the machine cannot go. We got the last load in today and have had no rain. Such luck! Indeed, it has been too hot even for me — it was 92° in the shade at eight o'clock this morning! We still have two and a half acres of excellent oats to cut and haul and then all our troubles are over for this Summer. The "Gloire de Dijon" rose got maggot-fly badly, but we sprayed it with a diluted solution of Carlo's precious home-made berry wine – and it worked! I always knew that he was poisoning us with the stuff!

We are thinking of taking a short holiday in September to visit the Horse Show in Victoria in order to look at Percherons and Clydesdales. Gerald and Faith will keep an eye on this place in our absence. For weeks, they have taken over the care of Claudia, except for Sundays, when we meet at Church and then take her home with us for the day.

The photographer came up from Victoria the other

day to take photos of Gerald and Faith's place. She will send you a photo as soon as she receives the copies. He took a group of us all on the front porch, Gerald with Faith, Carlo with Claudia and myself. I hope that it comes out well, the house and all of us. We wore our best Sunday bibs and tuckers on a boiling hot Thursday afternoon. We three men were freshly bathed and shaved for this important occasion. I decided to shave off my beard and only keep my moustache, so that you would recognise me!

My best love to you all. Take great care of your arm. When will the splint be removed?

Yr. affec. Son,
William

The Fens.   2nd July, 1910

My dear Mother,

I do hope that you are well and that your arm is giving you less trouble. It will take some time to heal properly, I'm afraid. You must be very patient and not over-do things. My letter-writing has become spasmodic but it has been such a busy Spring and Summer, and really I have had no news of any interest to tell you.

Do you remember Uncle Harold telling us that his firm on Tyneside was busy building a new vessel for the Canadians? It is the *Prince Rupert*, over 3,000 tons and travelling at 18 knots, a luxurious ship. She will ply twice weekly between Seattle and Prince Rupert, calling in at Vancouver. We all hope to get over to the coast from where we can see her pass by on her maiden voyage this month. A great excitement for this part of the world.

You asked about Charles and his future. I think that he will leave school next year when he will be eighteen. He may go in for survey work, as George has some influence there, but I do not know. In the scholastic line, he has achieved simply nothing at all and is bottom in all subjects. It is a waste of your money to keep him any longer at school. Strange to say, he has developed into a real town lad and longs to be living in a big city.

As I feel that there is no future for me on this place, I have been on the look-out lately for some suitable land for myself, as I would like to get started working during the Winter months on it, when outside paid work is scarce. I have had an exceedingly good offer of a strip of fifteen acres from our Reeve, Alec Aitkin. It is a mile further from Duncans than we are here, has an acre of lake frontage, two and a half acres of pasture, (no stumps), the rest is slashed, (that is, the trees cut down and the brush cut), and the soil is good, as rich as at "The Fens". The present owner wants 150 dollars an acre for it. Most land is now at 175 or 200 dollars and not even cleared. This is really an opportunity. I have been advised by men who have been out here all their lives.

I think that you are still holding Buenos Railway Stock for me? Would it be possible to sell this stock and to advance me the balance? Or I could pay you 5% interest if you give me a loan. That is the usual rate out here, and I will pay you back as the place begins to make a profit. Would that be better? I need, in English money, about £450 altogether. I hate to ask you, after all that you have done for me, but land is going up so much in price it will cost double in a year or two. If you can find your way to help me, could you cable me and I will close with the offer right away? I have saved over $100 from my work this year and could bind the owner with this sum, as a deposit, before anyone else has the chance to step in. You see, as this property, "The Fens", comes to George and Charles, why should I go on killing myself over it, just for them? I *must* get my own place. I cannot go on here any longer. I have reached the end.

Everyone sends their kind regards.

Ever Yr. affec. Son,

William

Monday, 3rd July.

Over the weekend, I decided not to risk losing this offer and have today paid over the sum of $100, as a deposit payment on the land. There were three other men after the property but I beat them to it! Gerald has just ridden over to tell me the splendid news that Faith gave birth to a son and heir, at 8:30 a.m. this very day! He weighs 7 lbs. 4 ozs. and will be christened John Gerald William and I have been asked to be one of the two godfathers!

The Fens.   10th Sept., 1910

My dear Mother,

Thank you very much for your great kindness in advancing the purchase money for my land.

I received the draft and have settled everything with Aitkin and paid him the money. I enclose the form for transfer of the shares, duly signed and witnessed as was directed in your letter.

Aitkin and I had a big burn of the whole sixty acres, of which my fifteen acres is a part. We had McRae and

Pooley to help us for the first three days and since then have managed by ourselves. It was very successful, burning slowly and thoroughly as the days were hot and calm. We had some anxious times and have been at it practically day and night, as, if it had got away into the bush, we might have burned miles of country. It was started a fortnight ago and is still smouldering, but quite safe now. I have been burning odd pieces that were missed, (there are always some), and branches, brush and as much rubbish as I can. I am then going to seed it down on the cold ashes with grass seed and clover, so as to get a good start of pasture. The rains will wash the seed in. Then, during the Winter, chop and saw all the smaller logs and poles and burn them in log piles, leaving the big trees for cordwood (firewood). If the weather is fairly fine, I ought to get the land looking like something by the Spring. Before the grass begins to come up, I shall have to fence of course, otherwise Aitkin's cows will pull up all my young shoots.

I should have several tons of hay off my field by late next Summer. It is sowed in Timothy Grass and Red Clover. Two Scottish brothers named Gardner have taken fifteen acres next to me. They seem very nice fellows. We had a lot of big trees come down on the bush line during the fire. Luckily nobody was hurt. We saw them coming and cleared out just in time.

Pooley won four firsts at the Duncans' Show with his chickens. You may remember that we built a studio for Carlo on his place? He showed two paintings in a Show down at Duncans recently and won prizes for both. A fine start!

I am not taking a holiday as I cannot afford it. Carlo will go to Victoria for a couple of days to the Horse Show there.

THE SECOND YEAR

Poor Mr and Mrs McRae have lost their first baby, a little girl, only a fortnight ago. McRae did not want either a Chinaman or an Indian to dig the grave and he was far too upset to do it himself, so I dug it for them. I was only too glad to do anything I could for them. They have been so brave about this loss. Mrs McRae was very ill but is now much better. It is a tough life for the women out in these parts.

I must stop now. It is long past my bed-time.

My best love to you all and thank you for all your goodness to me.

Yr. affec. Son,
William

The Fens.   6th November, 1910

My dear Mother,

I am sorry not to have written before but I do not seem to have had much time on my hands. It was very good of you indeed to send me such a handsome cash present which will cover the transfer and registration fees for my land. The present owner pays for the survey. When the weather is fine, I am very busy up at my place, sawing and chopping trees and logs into lengths of twelve feet or thereabouts, so that I can pile and burn them. It is a slow job and requires plenty of patience and perseverance, which I have learnt out here. Everyone thinks that it will be very nice, when I have cleared it. I am so happy again. For months and months I have not felt so bucked up, even though I am working quite alone up here.

Carlo and Gerald have been building another chicken-house and also the very first Motor Garage, for Mr Whittome, our big estate agent, who lives down near to the Church. Duncans starts to be really go-ahead! We are moving with the times!

I am so glad that you liked the photo which Faith sent you of us all. Yes, I have indeed lost a lot of weight since you last saw me, about three stone, actually, and I do know that my hair is pretty sparse on top. I was hoping that you would not notice this. I wanted to wear my panama hat, but the photographer said that it shaded my face too much.

The side of the house, with its broad verandah to the south and the sloping mansard roof, is really attractive, especially now that the climbing roses have begun to establish themselves. We took good cuttings from all the ones at "The Fens". Faith and Gerald's son, John, thrives apace and is always smiling and chuckling and taking an interest in everything. Claudia is delighted with her little "brother" and they share what was her room. In fact, she insists on doing everything with him and he adores her. She is now living all the time there, which I think that Antonia had hoped would happen.

There is little news from here. A friend, young Robinson, married Miss Phillipps-Wolley and the wedding went off very well and it was a most pretty one, on a sunny if rather cold day. I gave them six silver Apostle tea-spoons, the only spoons that they had given to them, so I was in luck.

George has finished his job on the road and is now trying to get into the draughtsmen's department in the Government Buildings in Victoria. I hope that he will get the post.

It has stopped raining now and I must get up to my

place to work, although it is bitterly cold and the under-growth is wringing wet. I take my lunch with me but always get back in time for the second milking.

To be able to write those two words, "my place", makes me feel a completely new fellow!

I know that this year, 1910, is the turning-point of my life!

My best love to you all.

Yr. affec. Son,

William

THE THIRD YEAR
1911

The Fens.   23rd January, 1911

My dear Mother,

Thank you for your kind wishes for Christmas and the New Year and also for your present of the very generous Money Order. Most useful, at this time.

I have not written for a long time because I had a very bad hand and can still only hold a pen between my thumb and little finger. I nearly lost three of my fingers in the bush. My saw was wet and slipped. Tasty food for the bears! Actually, they only got the tip of my second left finger, which has gone forever. It happened at dusk. I was all alone at the time so it was not very amusing.

I enclose the form which you sent me so as to complete the transfer of my Buenos Aires shares to your name, signed as requested. Thank you for all the trouble and expense which this has entailed, but now I have been able to pay our Reeve for my land, plus the 5% interest, which I had owed him on the purchase money since last August. Luckily he trusted me. At least out here I have a good name.

You have asked for my opinion about the situation here, about George, Charles and the property, but as Father had already written to Carlo (and long before you wrote to me), I cannot see that my opinion is of any value to you. I must say that I feel very hurt about this. However, I will give you the facts which it seems were not clear enough in Carlo's answering letter.

Charles takes no interest in the place whatsoever,

except to use it as a weekend house and a shooting-box. You can abandon any ideas which you may have had of seeing in him a successful future farmer and good property-owner. Any more of your money spent on his education would be pouring money down the drain, as he is too lazy to learn anything. He is, basically, a nice lad, but completely spoiled by his doting father. Each year, I am more bitterly disappointed in him. It can be, of course, that he has not as yet found the right outlet for his energies and is simply bored.

Carlo is definitely returning to Italy at the end of May. He is telling everyone that it is only for a visit but he and I know that he will never come back. He has become so unhappy that it is a good thing. We are all at logger-heads. It makes no sense to try to keep this place as a going concern except, of course, for the sake of getting a good selling price. As Father bought the property for Antonia and George in the first place, I feel that he should appoint George to arrange a sale and before Carlo leaves the country, as he and I, in our capacities as trustees, can help George. We would both gladly do that, for your sakes.

I have been trying to hold a property together which no one actually wants. As you well know, I am not in the position to continue to run a place as expensive as this one on my own and, even if the property were to be offered to me on a silver plate, I would not accept it. I do not wish to stay on here. Most definitely not! The last two years here have eaten into me as the previous years ate into Antonia. I understand her so much more now. How bitterly we both have had to pay for our one mistake! You were always very hard on her, Mother, but now that I know George and realise what she went through, alas! the facts have proved that you were right. Father was right, too, to judge me so harshly. I cannot talk with George and Carlo. I am all bottled-up and only breathing freely when I am up on my own place. What a great difference that makes, to be working on one's own soil with one's own dirty, torn hands! I wonder if you can understand that feeling? At home in England, everything is so long established, so immaculately organised, the wheels oiled and everyone in his or her place.

Something had to happen here and Carlo's definite departure is the ultimatum which we all needed.

On my own property, I think that I can go on – alone.
Yr. affec. Son,
William

"Oakleigh"   10th March, 1911

My dear Son,

Thank you for your last letter and I hope that your hand has completely healed. You must be in a very healthy physical condition indeed, as you mentioned no after-effects or poisoning. The climate must suit you, after all, in spite of your frequent grumbles.

I cannot imagine why you should have felt slighted by my letter. Of course your Father wrote to Mr Ghirlandi first. He is the senior of you two trustees and, in any case, he has known the circumstances at "The Fens" far longer than you have. However, your comments were also of value and bore out the information that we have already gathered – also from the lawyer. You seem to forget that we are having to assess a most difficult and complicated situation from a very great distance. Not only is there a large financial sum involved, but also the future of several members of our family.

Mr Ghirlandi had written to your Father before Christmas, to inform us that he was considering returning to Italy in the Spring and so your Father wrote to ask him for his opinions. He replied most clearly and helpfully and seems most desirous to assist us in every way, before he finally leaves the country. He has always behaved in a most correct manner.

Your last letter of 23rd Jan. shows us only too clearly that you yourself have no interest in continuing to live at "The Fens" and, last Summer, in your letter of 2nd July you asked me for assistance in obtaining farmland for your own future. Now I have complied with your wishes, taken over your good Buenos Aires Stock which your Father had given you and I sent you the £500 to cover the cost of the land-purchase and the transfer fees. I felt that you had handled this very hastily and without enough calm forethought. You never even waited for our opinion and simply presented us with a *fait accompli.* You will never learn to control your life with prudence and wisdom.

In view of these recent developments, your Father and I have decided to put the property on the open market, and we have engaged the services of a lawyer in Victoria to assist George in all practical and legal matters. We were biding our time as, at one moment, it seemed that George would contact us and propose that we should hand over the property to you. We would then, of course, have come to some financial arrangement with him, but you rushed your fences. Of course, we wish you to stay on and care-take the property until it is sold and the new owners can take over.

I think that you would like to know that we have donated an Altar Cloth and Hangings and a Chalice for the new Lady Chapel, in memory of Antonia. The Service of Dedication and Consecration was most beautifully conducted by the Bishop, assisted by our Rector. The Bishop and his sister (he is a widower), came to luncheon afterwards. We had eight other guests and all have written such charming letters of thanks, each with a special reference to their memories of Antonia. It is really quite extraordinary what a lasting impression she made on everyone whom she met. After all, it is now over twenty years since she left the country.

Last week, I had another nasty fall, in the garden, when I slipped backwards on the stone steps leading to the lower vegetable garden. Luckily your Father was on the terrace and heard my cries for help. Dr Martin came over at once, but nothing was broken and I have only sprained my left wrist and lacerated my hands and also have a large Belladonna Plaster on my bruised back, which I must keep on for six weeks.

The bad news seems to have spread quickly, as not only all my local friends called but also Mrs Alfred Diggles drove over from Bramhall and Mrs Booth from Fulshaw. I was most touched.

Your Aunt Agatha wrote to commiserate with me. She had most kindly sent your Father a barrel of oysters for his birthday on 20th Feb. So very generous of her and much appreciated. Her oysters in February and your Brother Arthur's brace of pheasants for my birthday in October are two of the most enjoyable annual events.

Aunt Bella joins me in good wishes to you. She has been very busy lately, repairing all the worn-out Ancient and Modern Hymn-books with paste and new book-linen. Last week, she discovered a £20 note in one of the four library books which we had ordered from Mudie's. After praying for guidance, we decided to give the money to the Mission to Seamen.

I do hope that you will now make a real success of your own farming efforts, now that you have got what you wanted.

Ever Yr. affec.
Mother

The Fens.   18th April, 1911

My dear Mother,

Thank you for your last letter. What bad luck you had and how unfortunate and painful such a fall can be. You have, indeed, been in the wars, one accident after another. What a mercy that Father heard your cries for help! All my sympathy.

Here things are gradually breaking apart. George has got that job in the Government draughters' office in Victoria and is now living in rooms in the town. He came home last weekend and tells us that he will now earn $80 a month and he seems to like the work. Charles has started a job in the "A.B.C. Motor and Marine" motorworks in Vancouver. He seemed more fitted for that type of job than for anything else. Cars are his passion. He started at $25 a month and has already risen to $30 in a short time. Mr Longhurst, a friend of ours, is one of the directors. He and his wife have been very good in looking after Charles, who has a comfortable room in their house and all his meals with them. I am happy that he has found his niche.

Carlo starts off for Italy somewhere about 24th May. This last Winter, he added a bedroom and a kitchen to his studio shack and so, when the home is sold, (and the "To be Sold" boards are now up and the place advertised in the Cowichan and Victoria papers), he and I will move in there together for a time, until he leaves. He will then transfer the shack into my name and it will be mine. He is truly a most generous chap. Lately, our relationship has become a real friendship.

Now I am hoping to sell five acres at the back of my land for about $200 an acre and then I will have the cash to build a small house and a barn, (suitable for two cows), and the fencing with the proceeds. I do not need those five acres. Ten is quite as much as I can cultivate alone. I reckon to have about three acres of hay, Timothy and Red Clover, ready to get in about July. I am now busy logging the others, (about seven acres), which I intend to keep. It is seeded with Blue Grass and Clover and seems to have caught pretty well.

I bought the heifer, "Holly", off George as a two-year old. She had a calf at Christmas (which is of course mine too), and is now in full milk. She is half Holstein, half Jersey, the calf is nearly all Jersey with a drop of Ayrshire and should be better than her mother. If all goes well, I should build the barn first so as to be ready for the hay, and then the house and fencing and take my cow and calf across there as soon as the grass has grown again after haying. Do you approve of what I am thinking of doing? If not, I will do whatever you think is better. I should sell the milk, of course, (we are doing so now), and eventually keep about thirty hens and sell eggs as well.

THE THIRD YEAR

163

So sorry to trouble you with such a long rigmarole about myself.

My best love to you all.

Yr. affec. Son,

William

The Fens.   21st May, 1911

My dear Mother,

Thank you very much for your last letter. Charles seems to be getting on alright. It was definitely the right thing to do to take him away from school at Easter and he seems happy over in Vancouver and enjoys city life.

As I wrote, the property has been advertised for sale for a month in both the Victoria paper, the *Colonist*, and also in the Cowichan paper and through our local house-agent in Duncans, Mr Whittome.

Carlo leaves for Italy on Tuesday morning, going home by the lakes. He is busy packing all his things now. I have given him my sea-chest and various cases and a hamper, for I will never need them again. He is travelling with our Station Agent, who has a long leave, and they are joining up with a group who are going over for the Coronation of our new King George and Queen Mary. That promises to be a great event. Their boat sails on 2nd June from New York.

Several people have already been looking over the place, but no one has taken it yet. Two prospective buyers decided on smaller places with less land. This has become a tremendous district for retired army men, chiefly from the Indian Army. They are a dried-up, liverish, dyspeptic-looking lot but they seem to like this area. It is indeed very beautiful. They will find that their former military ranks cut little ice in these parts, where everyone is known by his first name and where class distinctions count for nothing. Only Nature decides who are the "gentlemen". You need physical endurance and a very large portion of humour to get along over here.

Of course I shall stay on until the property sells. Did I tell you that Carlo is handing over the shack and all its contents to me as his parting present? — most generous of him. It is a great relief to me to have somewhere to live. I shall miss him very much. In the last months, we have become really firm friends. How quickly the situation has altered for all of us. Carlo was the catalyst in all our lives.

I am sorry to realise that I have missed your birthday. I have never been a good son. Please try to forgive me.

Bed now, as I must rise at 5 a.m. tomorrow for my creamery day.

Yr. affec. Son,
William

The Fens.   23rd May, 1911

My dear Aunt Bella,

I feel that I must write to you and share with you these last few weeks of my life here at "The Fens", knowing that you will understand me.

I have never mentioned this before but it touched me very deeply that it was you and Father who became ill with worry after my disgrace. Mother just squared her shoulders, stuck out that famous jaw of hers and carried on. But you *knew*, you were not blind and, although we never had a chance to talk together, I felt that you somehow understood me and knew the problems that a fellow like me has to face. Mother was always lining up socially suitable young ladies for me. I think that you knew all along that I am not the marrying type. It is all so hard to explain.

Now I have just returned from seeing Carlo Ghirlandi off for the last time. I drove him to the station in the buggy (almost as fully loaded as when I arrived here), and Gerald, Faith and Claudia were waiting for us at the station. It was a very hard farewell, especially when I held Claudia to the train window for the last kiss and hug. How lucky that she did not understand just what this parting meant to all of us! She has a new family life with the Carruthers, to all of whom she is devoted, especially to little John. Carlo gave her a Labrador puppy as a farewell present. It is strange, she never mentions either George or Charles, but often talks of her mother almost as if she were there in the room. I gave her the photograph that I had of Antonia for her last birthday. It is in a nice leather frame. I could not bear to have it around me anymore. When Claudia once asked me why she had to die when she was so much loved, I could only burst into tears and tell her that only God knew the answer. What can one say to a small child? My own loneliness and bitterness can only be kept to myself.

The house is unbelievably empty now. No laughter, no sudden explosions of Italian temperament around the place. I even miss the permanent smell of onions! Our last months together were just like the old days when Antonia was alive. Carlo had also been living on here under great strain. In my ignorance, I could not fully appreciate just what he had gone through. Then, suddenly, one snow-bound weekend last Winter, we talked everything out and since then there have been no secrets between us. He trusts me and I can trust him, always. This will be a surprise to you, as it was to me, but he had a wonderful relationship with Antonia – they were lovers. After her death, I suppose I was jealous of him whenever he talked about her, for he knew her so much better than I did. I do so wish that I had understood earlier. That Winter weekend, I laid all my cards on the table too and he, being an artist, understood just what a stupid, muddled sort of fellow I am and the sort of close friendship with another man for which I am searching. I wish that we could both have trusted the other far sooner.

Carlo will miss Claudia so much. She was all that he had left of that wonderfully passionate relationship with Antonia, but it is better for them both this way, for he could never have brought Claudia up alone and he cannot bear to think of marrying. Luckily, she has inherited her mother's dark beauty and so no one will ever ask questions or have doubts about her real parentage.

I have never respected Carlo as much as I do now and I am thankful to know that Antonia had those few, last, joyous years with him in his devoted company, whatever the difficulties and the scruples – and that they had Claudia to share. I have to thank him that we parted today as real friends. He is my true brother-in-law, not George.

Please keep this letter to yourself. It is not to be answered, for it is only the over-flowing thoughts of a fellow sitting by his fire with a mug of beer – alone. God bless you, dear Aunt, and keep you well and in good spirits.

Ever Yr. loving Nephew,
William

THE THIRD YEAR

The Fens.   25th May, 1911

My dear Mother,

I have little news for you. I do not see many people now and had not been down into Duncans for over three months until last Tuesday, when I went to see Carlo Ghirlandi off to Italy. A sad day.

Now I number among my milk clients a Chinaman, who is the cook in a logging camp near here, and also two Sikhs. The Sikhs are brothers and fine fellows. They have both been army men in India and are saving up to go back there and farm their own land. They tell me that their family owns 200 acres back home. Our conversations are in signs and Pidgin English and would amuse you. They are very polite and always salute me as a white sahib – me, this skinny, mahogany-faced freak in dirty overalls and with a workman's worn hands!

I went with McRae and his wife to see his wife's parents, Mr and Mrs Kingston, last night, and heard all the scandal of the entire neighbourhood from the old lady, who is a very hard-working busybody. Her old husband is a fine Irishman, as deaf as a post. He shouts at you and you nod and smile and wave your arms about to show that you appreciate what the old gentleman is yelling about.

Why am I writing this letter? It cannot possibly interest you, in Cheshire.

Thank you again for your great goodness to me.

I am trying to be worthy of it.

My best love to all.

Yr. affec. Son,

William

My dear Mother,

    Thank you very much indeed for your kind birthday letter and for the very handsome Money Order. I have been much occupied at "The Fens", with people coming to view the place, taking hours and hours of my time and then going away, undecided. Thank Heavens that the Burns family from Alberta have finally clinched the deal, and now things just have to run their course. I have promised them to stay on here and run the place until they can take it over, which will not be before they have got their own last harvest in Alberta in. They will take over on 1st September or October – depending on the harvest time. After that, they have kindly said that I may stay on in Carlo's shack until my own place is ready and not to hurry. Very decent of them. I think that your property will be in the hands of people who will appreciate it. That should please you both. So, now I can concentrate all my energy and thoughts on my own place. I have already been very busy sawing up blocks and collecting rocks for the foundations of my barn and hope to start building it in a week or so, but the weather has been so hot and dry that I will have to get my hay in first, stack it and load it later into the new barn, after I have built it. Rather putting the cart before the horse, but it cannot be helped.

    The value of my land is going up and I have been offered $250 an acre of land for it. You will remember that I paid $150 an acre only last year. Of course, I have no intention of selling. As you have very kindly offered to pay for the building and setting-up of my place, I want to tell you what I propose building – a house of four rooms, that is, a living-room 15 ft. by 12 ft., two bedrooms, each 10 ft. by 12 ft. and a kitchen 15 ft. by 12 ft. and with an 8-foot verandah, to overlook the lake. If you think my plans too grand, please say so, and I will cut them down. The reason for the second bedroom is that I would like a guest-room, in case anyone ever comes out on a visit to me from home, and also for Claudia. When she comes over for a day, she could stop the night. I want to make a real home atmosphere here. I will not start building until August, so there will be plenty of time for alterations if you deem them necessary.

I was worried by your last letter and hearing that you now suffer so much from neuralgia in your head. I did not realise that you had hit your head so badly when you had your last fall. Please take great care of yourself.

The Carruthers send their best wishes. He and I are still selling our milk to Chinamen, Hindoos and other camp folk. Pooley has told me how they all came to be living in these parts. A few Chinese came up from California in the Gold Rush of 1858, but most of them came over from China to work on the railroad construction in the 80s and then settled here. They say that the Hindoos went over to England, via the Suez Canal from India in 1887, to take part in the celebrations for Queen Victoria's Jubilee. They then travelled back to India across Canada, and were so attracted to British Columbia that many returned later, bringing their families with them, and got work in the mines and in the lumber camps. I find them both, Chinese and Hindoos, good and honest customers. They do not drink hard liquor, which is the plague of the Indians, but what a disgraceful example *we* set them!

I sold 276 quarts of milk to the camps last month and

had skim milk for Gerald's chickens and for my calf, as well as plenty of milk for our home use. Pretty good for only two cows!

My best love to you all. No more news.

Yr. affec. Son,

William

The Fens. 30th June, 1911

My dear Mother,

Thank you very much for your kind letters received. The draft has arrived safely. I am very grateful to you and to Father for your great kindness in helping me to build my own house and this is just a quick acknowledgement note, as I am going down to Duncans straight away to bank the $1,000.

I will write longer letters to answer all your questions and tell you the latest news. I am expecting Charles over to spend a week's holiday with me here in The Fens, for the very last time. He will then pack up the personal things that he still has here and take them over with him to Vancouver, where he now has rented rooms of his own. He is doing very well.

Tomorrow is Cowichan Bay Regatta and a public holiday. We are all going.

Yesterday, I was busy cooking cakes and puddings and pies for Charles' arrival.

Please give everyone my love.

Yr. affec. Son,

William

PS. Please excuse this paper. I am out of writing-paper

at present. This grease-proof paper is what we make the butter up in!

CABLE
Dated 1st August, 1911 9:15 a.m.

```
YOUR FATHER DEPARTED THIS LIFE
YESTERDAY AFTER A BRIEF ILLNESS STOP
LETTER FOLLOWS STOP
MOTHER
```

Carlo's Shack,
Duncans Station.   2nd Aug., 1911

My dear Mother,

I have just received your cable with the sad news and have been down to Duncans at once, to cable my deep condolences to you. I am so very very sorry for you. I think that Father and you were just all in all to each other. You were never apart and you will miss him terribly. I only hope that he did not have to suffer. Your cable said, "Brief illness". I do wish that I could be with you in your great sorrow. I cannot realise that he has gone. I did long to make good out here on my own and had always secretly hoped that, one day, he might be able to forgive me and come out to see what I had achieved. Now that can never be. There was so much that I had planned to show him.

I cannot sleep at night for thinking of him and I lie listening to the owls and to the frogs in the marshes, waiting impatiently for the first cock-crow and the dawn, so that I can get up and start another heavy working-day.

Father was a man in ten thousand. I do not think that I shall ever meet anyone quite like him in my lifetime. Not only was he so handsome, even in old age, but one can hardly realise the great influence for good which he had on everyone with whom he came in contact. He really practised Christian charity in the true sense.

I hope that God will comfort you and that your religious Faith will help you to bear this great trial. He may have been taken to save him any further suffering or physical weakness, which a man of his strength of mind and body and soul should not have had to bear, not if there is any justice on this earth. God was indeed kind to him and to Antonia in taking them both so quickly to Him.

No doubt I shall hear from home in a week or two. I seem so very far away and completely cut off from you all, never lonelier than now, all by myself in the shack. Antonia is dead. Carlo is now in Italy. George is somewhere in the south on survey. Charles is over in Vancouver. Claudia is living with Faith and Gerald and now dear Father has gone, too.

I will write again soon, my dear Mother. God bless you and strengthen you.

I mourn with you all.

Yr. sorrowing and loving Son,
William

Dear Mr Newton-Lanes,

May we commiserate with you on the sad loss of your most deeply respected father, Mr Newton-Lanes.

His departure from our midst has robbed us of one of the most outstanding men in the Manchester legal and business world.

You may rest assured that my brother and I, not only in our function as his appointed solicitors, but also as his friends, will do all in our power to assist and support his widow, your mother, through this very distressing and difficult time.

Over two years ago, in January 1909, your father gave this sealed, private and confidential letter into our hands, to be forwarded to you only in the event of his demise.

We hereby enclose this letter and would appreciate an immediate acknowledgement of its safe arrival.

Assuring you of our most heartfelt condolences,

I remain, yours sincerely,

(*signed*) Gordon G. Locke (Senior partner)

Locke and Locke (Solicitors),
4, St Martin's Court, Haymarket, Liverpool

WILLIAM'S STORY

"Oakleigh"   9th January, 1909

My own very dear Son,

I am writing on my return home from seeing you for what I know was the very last time, waving your hat to me as your ship sailed away from the dock.

The writing of this letter will be the most difficult task of my life and, believe me, there have been very many testing situations in my span of over three score and ten. I have failed and I am a coward to send you this letter only after I am dead. If there was not always this unbridgeable *silence* between the generations, between the parents and their children! If only we could have spoken to each other much earlier, as I am now speaking to you, far too late.

Only in the past two weeks have I been enormously aware of what I represent to you – the authoritative father, the successful lawyer, the respected Justice of the Peace, the devout churchwarden, the enthusiastic president of the Sports' Association. What an oil-painting that represents and it hangs in our dining-room over the side-board.

In my dealings with both you two boys, I have been desperately conscious of only having given life to you. Nothing more. Then I left everything else to your Mother, to nurses, governesses, tutors, schools and colleges. In my relations with you, I simply extended my revolt against the world of my own parents.

This personal and indeed general revolt goes back far into the 19th century, because I think that, from then on, the *Homo Sapiens* developed so suddenly and with such an incredible increase in momentum, that we lost our way. Was it not Sir Richard Burton who gave us the old Arab aphorism: "A man's soul cannot travel faster than the pace of a running camel"? If we were not to be one of those crushed under the wheels of the infernal steam-machines that we were perfecting, then we quiescently stood by and oiled them. The new Midas touch.

So, in 1860, after coming down from Cambridge, I mutinied, made my one-man stand, quietly realised all I possessed, which was a small bank account, two thoroughbreds, a leather-bound library of meretricious taste, a gold watch and a signet ring and also, cowardly again, wrote a bald note to break off the engagement to the suitable fiancée, chosen by two business-affiliated fathers. I knew, at least, that this girl would be as relieved as I was, for she loved another and much finer man.

I left Huddersfield secretly, and sailed steerage to the Argentine. My parents, most correctly, disowned me. I had been brought up and educated to inherit all those machines, all those grinding wheels, but unknown to all those in authority, I had unfortunately read Cobden and Blake.

Now you will understand why I knew exactly what your requirements would be in a pioneer land, and could advise your Mother as to what would be welcomed birthday and Christmas presents. I ran away. You were sent away. There is little factual difference between us. You are the son of your father.

Docking, after weeks at sea, in Buenos Aires, I obtained a clerking situation with an English firm of importers and set about learning the language. About two years later, I travelled up the River Plate, and found work as a cattleman on three different ranches, in order to gain the indispensable experience for running a property of my own. I needed to get back to the land, any land, any earth anywhere, but earth that belonged to me, to be worked by my hands.

WILLIAM'S STORY

More than twenty-five years passed. You are still too young to know how a quarter of a century can vanish in one night through a single unpremeditated decision.

I was forty-five years old when my parents, your grandparents, were killed, drowned when a ferry-boat collided in a fog and sank in the Irish Sea.

Then I made the greatest mistake of my life. Out of false piety and delusions of remorse, I returned to England to visit their graves, bringing Antonia with me. Yes, she is only your half-sister. Her most wonderful and darling mother, of Spanish descent, died at her birth. It was she who made a man out of me.

After attending Mattins in our old Church, the service which embraced the special prayers of remembrance for my parents, which I had arranged with the Rector, I was fortuitously introduced to your Mother. We were married three months later. She was a childless widow and I was a widower with one child.

Only on our Honeymoon did she bluntly announce that she had no intention whatsoever of returning with me to an unknown ranch on an unknown river in South America.

You know your Mother. I sold the ranch, without ever seeing it again, bought this property, which she chose, and returned to the profession which had been originally planned for me, the Law of Business, and allowed myself to be moulded by your Mother into a model of social excellence, business acumen and domestic propriety. I was simply too tired to fight back. Too much of my youthful strength and all my idealism were buried in that very dry earth of the Plate Valley. You will not understand, perhaps, how a grown-up man can suddenly cave in. I buried myself in work.

THE THIRD YEAR

So you were born, nine months after our Wedding-day and Arthur a year later. Your Mother very nobly kept my secret and let you think that Antonia was your much older sister. Your Mother is a very fine woman.

Antonia was a most remarkable child and a brilliant girl. She had inherited much more from Toledo than from Huddersfield! Completely understanding her Step-mother, she herself was utterly misunderstood. So she left us, for her "emigration", like her father before her. She went the only way that was possible for someone in her position – married, to George Carfax, who also wanted to leave the country for reasons of his own. So she, too, travelled westwards, as I had done before her.

My dear dear Son, this is my apology to you for having failed you when you most needed me, and Antonia too. Having married your Mother, I had to fit into the role for which she had cast me. I admit that I have done that most successfully, but I have handed on to you only my own spoiled youth, my weaknesses, my romanticism and my indecisions. If you had only felt that you could come to me and confess that you had stolen, in order to pay the black-mailing sums to that wicked man, I would have understood you, however wrongly you had behaved. For illicit passion is expensive.

Please try to forgive me and to believe that I have suffered and have been convicted. You, I could help to avoid prison. Myself, I condemned to a life sentence.

May God bless you, my Boy, and give you the strength to make your own way. That is what life is all about. One day you will find yourself and then you will understand.

Your very sad and loving

Father

Dated 20th August, 1911 3:30 p.m.

YOUR DARLING MOTHER PASSED AWAY
PEACEFULLY TODAY STOP
PNEUMONIA STOP LETTER FOLLOWS TODAY
STOP
AUNT BELLA

Carlo's Shack,
Duncans Station.   2nd Sept., 1911

My dear Aunt Bella,

    Thank you so much for your cable and for the kindest letter which anyone could ever have written. Everything has happened so quickly. I am only glad that Mother received the letter in time that I had written to her, directly after hearing of Father's sudden death, and that my words had made her happy and had comforted her.

    It must all be a great shock to you, the sudden departure of Father and then to be bereft of your sister, and both in less than a month. Your account of everything was most clear and helpful to me. I am glad that dear Father was spared any suffering and that his heart simply gave out in his sleep. As for Mother, doubtless her several falls and breakages had weakened her and then the final blow of Father's death will have brought on this fatal attack of pneumonia.

    Thank you for describing the two funerals so clearly and for sending wreaths in my name. The wording on the two cards was perfect, just what I would have written myself. You are so kind and thoughtful. I can visualise the place in the Churchyard where they are buried together, but I will never see it with my own eyes, nor put flowers on their graves with my own hands.

I did long to be with Father again. Did you know that he left a letter for me with Locke and Co., the lawyers, to be sent to me at his death? One day I may have the strength to tell you about it. Not now, for my heart is bursting. It was a wonderful letter.

You will see from the address that I am now living in Carlo's old place. Since last week, I have been very busy, packing up all the furniture and things from "The Fens", as Charles is miles away on the mainland and George is on survey, somewhere on the Island. I did it all with grand help from Faith and Mrs Aitkin. They were real trumps.

The new owners, Mr and Mrs Burns and their family from Alberta, have brought all their own furniture from their former home on the prairies and, of course, wanted a cleared and cleaned house to move into. I got two Chinese women to help me. The Burns have brought their own stock, too. So now all our things have been moved over to the house which George has bought, with 100 acres of land. It all seems an idiotic waste for practically nothing, but it seems that he always loathed it here. Of course, now I know why. It is ironical that he did get "The Fens" in the end. Mother died on the 20th August and the contract for the property was only signed by Mr Burns and the money handed over on the 25th! That really makes me boil, that George should have had the last laugh.

I wanted some small mementos of the old home and George let me have Antonia's little bureau and her rocking-chair, and also one of her water-colours of the house, covered in roses. Also one of Carlo's oils, a lovely view, looking away from the house towards the lake at sunset. It is the landscape which we all enjoyed together, for such a short time, that unique light on the marshes and a dark bird or two, winging home.

I have been very busy getting my hay in, making a road to my place. McRae helped me. He owed me a fortnight's work. We had a very tough job, about half a mile, for there were many stumps to blow out and much levelling to be done. We have just finished and now start on the fencing. It is a wonderful "Indian Summer" and ideal for working. I shall have to build a much larger barn than planned as my hay harvest was far heavier than I had reckoned. I want to get it finished by October, when the nights get cold, and then I can house my stock. My old friend, "Holly" and her daughter, "Berry", have come with me.

There is so much work to do that I cannot build my house this year, so I shall just put up a woodshed-cum-toolshed and live there this Winter. I have to hand over this shack to the new-comers at "The Fens" as soon as possible. All the furnishings are, of course, mine – from Carlo. However, I can stay on here until I have a roof over my head. But, nothing is wasted. I would have had to build a shed anyway.

The Summer has been a very long, hot and dry one this year. It is 98° in the shade today and we are bathed in perspiration. Our haying season has lasted about two months altogether. We ourselves got in about eighty loads. The weather was so favourable that everyone in the neighbourhood has enjoyed a good harvest.

This is a tremendous lot about myself. I find it so easy to write to you. When Mother was alive, I realised that any letter that I wrote to you only provoked her jealousy. So I kept my letters down to the minimum — just at Christmas and for your birthday. I knew that you understood. May I write regularly to you now? You are my only link with the Old Country.

I have never heard from Arthur again and not received one single letter from any of my old so-called friends. Well, I have built up a new life over here, with one or two real friends, not just fair-weather ones. I am often very lonely but I am breathing freely again, breathing in my own air under my own patch of sky, standing on my own land.

My fondest love to you, my dear Aunt.

Ever Yr. loving Nephew,

William

Carlo's Shack.   10th Dec., 1911

My dear Aunt Bella,

This is to wish you and your friends a very Merry Christmas and a Happy New Year. Thank you very much for your kind letter and for the Money Order, received safely. I wish that I could be with you on Christmas Day and be able to bring you some little gift in token of my appreciation for all that you have done for me since the parents died.

I will be with Gerald and his family. Charles suddenly turned up at my shack the other day. I had not heard a word from him since he stayed with me last July. He will, I hope, be going to visit his father in Victoria for Christmas but I do not yet know. Work seems to be very slack in his line at the moment and he also does not seem to hit it off with his parents-in-law. They want him to come into a Real Estate office, but he wants to stay in the motor trade. He is more fitted for the latter, I think. Did I tell you that he got married last October? I am quite sure that the girl's parents are not so very happy at having a nineteen-year-old for a son-in-law.

I am glad that two of your old friends are joining forces with you for the Christmas festivities. They will be a great comfort to you and you will not be alone in that big house, which I am truly happy to hear that you have inherited.

I had started my fencing and the work on the barn, but then we had two to three feet of new snow, which lay for three weeks and meant that I spent all my time getting to my stock just to feed and look after them. It was bitterly cold. The day following the first very heavy snowfall, it took me forty-five minutes just to walk the 400 yards to the stable. And then I had to climb in through the stable window! However, we have had a complete thaw since and so the fencing and the barn will be finished this week, with any luck, so I can move into my own place in time for Christmas.

Of course Mother was right, as usual, and I tore up my utopian plans for that four-roomed house and came down to earth with a bang. However, the cost of building materials has gone up a good deal lately and I will have spent nearly $500 (about £100 roughly), more than the sum which the parents sent me to build my home.

I do not like asking for more money, immediately after you have taken over the responsibility, and I could raise this sum by selling off part of the land. I feel that this would be a great pity. I am honestly doing all I can to earn money but the powers of one man by himself are limited. Please be sure to say if it is not possible. Probably you will have to consult the family lawyer?

We had a very large fire in Duncans the other day. In fact, the whole village would have been wiped out if the rain had not suddenly descended in torrents and helped put it out. It was really the Hand of God which saved them all down there. Everyone saw the flames and the smoke for miles around and got over to help, just as fast as they could. That sort of team-work is just magnificent. Several chaps got badly burned.

So my third year out here draws to a close. It seems more like twenty to me and I have certainly aged a score or more. You would not recognise me.

My fondest love to you, my dear Aunt,

Yr. loving Nephew,

William

THE FOURTH YEAR
1912

Skeecullus,
Duncans Station.   28th Feb., 1912

My dear Aunt Bella,

Thank you very much for your good wishes for Christmas and for the most useful and very strong Bedford-cord trousers. I have also received the two Money Orders safely and the cheque from the dividends on the shares which you hold for me. The receipts are herewith duly signed and witnessed, rather belatedly, I am afraid.

I do apologise that I have become such an erratic letter-writer, but there is simply nothing to write about. My life is one daily grind, broken only by my weekly ride into Duncans for the mail and a glass of beer. On Sundays, I join Gerald and his family at Church and am always invited back to their home for their Sunday dinner, and we enjoy a happy time with the children. Gerald and I drank to your health with a bottle of beer each at Christmas. Pooley very kindly invited me over for the evening and also Charles, who did not go home to his wife for Christmas. I do not know how that will work out. I do not ask questions nor give advice. My own problems keep me busy enough. He left me early in January and I have heard nothing since then.

The deep snows held my work up badly, so that I was only able to move into my new home on the 26th January. I did my "house-removal" from Carlo's shack to my new place in a blizzard, as I had hired a cart for that day and paid for it in advance and so could not afford to put things off. I have called my first home, "Skeecullus", which means "The Sad One". It has been founded on so much sadness. It is only a simple shack but it is *my home*, built with my own hands, my own unaided effort. This is my life now. I always wanted a place of my on and now I am in it, alone.

One of the reasons why I have not written earlier is that I have been rather in the wars. My calf, "Berry", got mixed with her mother, my old cow, "Holly", in her stall. I went to pull her out and somehow slipped, managing to break a rib, lacerate my chest muscles and strain my wrist. This story sounds very awful but it is really nothing much out here. These sorts of things amuse people more than anything else. You just give everybody the chance to have a really side-splitting laugh. I mend worse, as they say in Cheshire, but my chest and wrist have already healed and only my rib is still very tender. That reminds me of Sunday luncheons at home, with tender Sirloin of Beef, with three vegetables and Yorkshire pudding and rich gravy.

Since then, I have had an attack of dysentery. My water supply cannot be as pure as I thought and how lucky that Mother does not know that George now has her famous Water-filter, she would be furious! By the way, George has married again, so I hear, but that may only be a rumour.

My start in the new home has not been very auspicious, but Spring is on its way and the warmer weather, and the Dogwoods will bloom again.

No, my accent has not become in the least bit Canadian and, with my English wardrobe, (thanks to you all), I am still regarded very much as the English wag, which is a harmless enough role to live up to. A friend is coming over to take photographs of the place, myself and any other wild animals who might creep out of the bush. His charges are reasonable and far cheaper than that shark from Victoria. I will send you some copies.

One bit of news for you — there was a terrific celebration picnic for the Coronation last Summer, with venison steaks roasted on iron skillets, smoked salmon, jacket potatoes and simply gallons of tea and many kegs of beer. Now we have just heard that Duncans will become a City this year and will then direct its own affairs, independent from all those stiff-collared, stuffy officials in Victoria. So everyone is busy planning an even bigger affair for the Declaration of the City. It will be a simply fabulous do.

My wrist is petering out. Writing is rather a painful business but I did just want to send you my best love. I think it wise of you to sell up the old home and to look for something more manageable. With Arthur now enjoying his married life with Olivia and little Thomas and also his successful business career in Aberdeen, why should you try to hold the place together? I learnt that lesson the hard way. Please only think of yourself and of your own future. As the Parents bequeathed the property to you, you can do entirely what you want with it. Please do not consider either Arthur or me. We have made our own lives, for better or worse. I am glad that you have been able to discuss it with Arthur. He is a very fair and responsible man and will assist you all he can, of that I am sure. Do not hang on to the memories of the past, whether happy or sad. It would be perfect if you could get a pleasant house and a manageable garden together with your old school-friend. What about in your beloved Lake District? Is this a good idea of mine? Right away from the past!

Did I ever write that fens out here are called "sloughs"? How very appropriate that is. "The Fens" was my Bunyan's "Slough of Despond" indeed. I should have called this place "Hardgrind Farm", but I feel that "Skeecullus" will still be here, long after all the grind is over and I am dead and buried.

My best love to you and my kind regards to all your friends, especially to Miss Wheeler and good luck for your joint house-hunting.

Ever Yr. affec. Nephew,
William

THE FIFTH YEAR

1913

Skeecullus,
Duncans Station.   2nd March, 1913

My dear Aunt Bella,

Well, I have survived another year out here! I am a poor correspondent indeed. Thank you for all your letters and for the present for Christmas. Everything arrived safely, including the annual cheque from my dividends. You wrote rather sarcastically but justifiably in your Christmas letter that the least I can do is to send you an "Annual Report", even if my one-man firm seems to be permanently "in the red".

So, with this letter, I am enclosing the photo of my place, taken last Spring. I never sent it to you as I was rather ashamed to have to admit that all I had was a one-room, unheated shack. Since then, and after getting my hay in last year, I have built additions to the place, turning the former woodshed, (on the right of the photo and with a borrowed boat from McRae in it), into my bedroom and I have built a new, open-fronted stove in the room on the left, (you can see the old pipe sticking out of the wall), and now made this side into my living-room. The fire burns very well now, with a proper chimney, and the room is really cosy. The new woodshed is built onto the back of the shack, adjoining the toolshed. The large barn which I built first is way out of the picture and over to the right.

Also, I have cleared up and ploughed another acre of land nearer the lake, so that you can see that I am constantly

William on the steps of his shack at Skeecullus, holding Rufus

improving my property. I sold my old friend, "Holly" and also "Berry", her calf, for $100 and bought three nearly pure-bred Jersey cows, "Di" aged seven, "Maggie" aged four and "Ivy" aged three. I gave $250 for these jerseys and they have already paid for themselves. So I now have what in this country is called a "Milk Walk", and supply thirteen families around here with milk, my "Swiss" butter and cream. The profit is about $35 a month, after paying all expenses for the feed, (oats, etc.), for the cows, my horse and two pigs. I have a Yorkshire sow, too, and a young registered Berkshire boar. Now I hope for good litters as one can get $4 each as soon as the piglets are weaned. I was genuinely sorry to say goodbye to old "Holly", but saw that both she and "Berry" went to good homes. My reason for keeping Jerseys is that their calves fetch a much better price and also their surplus milk makes much better butter, and more in quantity.

Our Winter was very severe and I had to keep the stock inside the barn for over two months, owing to deep snow. My milk round took me over three hours instead of the usual one hour.

Now, as to my health, I am rather thin but very fit. I rise each day at 5:30 a.m. and do not finish work until I have given the stock their second meal at 9 p.m. I do not seem to be able to put on any flesh. Life is rather too strenuous for that, but I am considered the best bachelor cook in the district, so you need not worry about the "grub department"! Most bachelors' staple meals are of pork and beans or bacon and eggs, but I cook from Mother's, Antonia's and Carlo's cookery recipes and so have the best of English, Canadian and Italian recipes, although one needs quite a bit of fantasy to supply missing ingredients, but that is half the fun.

Will you now please send me a photograph or sketch of your new home, with as much of Scawfell as you can get into the picture? How often I climbed in those parts of the Lake District in the old days, with Father and Arthur, when we were boys. Your place sounds lovely. Your new neighbours charming, too. I also have a delightful new neighbour – a young Racoon, who lives in a hollow tree by my fence, down at the lake's edge. He spends all day climbing, swimming and sleeping. How I envy him! He always washes his food very carefully before he eats it. He's a comical little fellow and seems to be all on his own, a bachelor like me.

Also, I have a new hobby, astronomy. I found a map of all the planets and stars in a bundle of books that I bought in a sale and have great fun plotting the constellations, finding the North Star by using the pointers of the Dipper.

It is a fascinating hobby on a clear night, when one is alone and not able to sleep.

No, I never found another "Sheppy" but another "Rufus" found me! He is in the photo with his head poking through under my left arm. He is a grand little chap, a sort of bastard Bearded Collie, brown and white. He landed up on my steps on a rainy evening a year ago, starving and covered in thick, wet mud. He cleverly weighed up the situation and realised, most astutely, that our need for each other's company was entirely mutual. And so he decided to stay. He follows me everywhere. His owner must have moved away from the district and he got left behind, for I made enquiries all over the place. He was a trained dog and is very good with the stock.

Now that I have been living at "Skeecullus" for over a year, I have learnt to love the flow of the seasons. I am much more settled and find that I can live quite happily both with myself and with my surroundings. I have little social life, except for a glass of beer on a Saturday evening with friends, or an occasional fishing or hunting trip with Gerald or McRae. Always Church on Sundays and then dinner with Gerald, Faith, Claudia and John, and much fun playing with the children. With all the animals here, I am never alone. Also I pick up all the local news from the folk whom I visit on my milk walk and they all welcome me as a cheery dropper-in. Occasionally I'm asked to stop for a meal.

I have changed, fitting in here like a chameleon and you would probably not recognise, but I am still

Yr. affec. Nephew,
William

Skeecullus,
Duncans Station.   2nd April, 1913

My dear Aunt Bella,

"The boy must want something", you will be saying, to
write again so soon. Of course, you are right and I will not
beat about the bush. In your last letter, you asked me if I
had enough pasture now that I have more cows. No, I find
that I have not got enough land and, if my milk business
increases as it is doing at the present, I will be very short of
feed. I have been offered fifteen acres adjoining mine and
have accepted, subject, of course, to your consent because I
want you to sell my shares in order to raise the purchase
money.

The land belongs to friends of mine, two Scottish
brothers, who had intended living there but they have now

William's letter of 2nd April, 1913

THE FIFTH YEAR

decided to stay on in their present place, which is nearer to Duncans and civilisation. It takes me nearly an hour on horseback into town. They had already cleared about half the land, taken most of the stumps out but not levelled it. The price is $7,000 for the fifteen acres. Land has gone up greatly in value since I bought my present place and, considering the amount of work already done on the land, it is one of the cheapest buys on the market.

I have already made an advance to them in order to secure the land and am starting in at once to level it and to plough the first four acres in order to put in a crop of Oats. They have to be in in a week to ten days, otherwise it would be too late in the season. I hope that you do not think that I am again rushing matters, but it seemed the wisest thing to do. They have already fenced it – a good fine board fence and cedar posts, exactly like mine.

This is a dull and selfish letter but this new bit of property is taking up all my thoughts and time, not to mention my strength.

The weather is getting me down. Rain for days and days on end. It is like a slow Chinese torure, dripping endlessly, and the soaking wet undergrowth seems to thicken into impenetrable green bush as you look at it. Heavy mists cover the land as far away as you can see and the lake is invisible from my shack. No one rides over for a chat. Everyone is busy repairing leaking roofs or digging out channels to drain off the deep muddy pools around their homes and barns.

It is a fearful struggle to get through my milk walk, for the cart's wheels get stuck in the mire, my horse gets soaked and dispirited and the shack reeks of wet socks and sodden tweed. There seems no end to it. Nothing dries.

This is a foul mood in which to write what was meant to be a letter to congratulate you on the very first home of your own. We started together! May you be a very happy house-owner up in the Lake District and please give my kind regards to your friend, Miss Wheeler.

My best love, dear Aunt,

Yr. affec. Nephew,

William

Skeecullus,
Duncans Station.   21st May, 1913

My dear Aunt Bella,

I am sorry to hear that you have had influenza and hope that you are now completely recovered and able to enjoy life again. So much lying in bed must have been very trying for you, especially in lovely Spring weather. I am writing this sitting in the sun on my front steps, and a Robin has just dropped an eggshell on my head! You know that the parent birds always fly well away from their nest with the empty shells, in order to conceal the whereabouts of their baby-birds, but why choose me as a decoy?

You asked about the extra land. I think I wrote to you early in April that it would cost $7,000. Much of it was cleared and that makes it the cheapest buy anywhere around here. Land at the lakes is selling for $700 to $1,000 an acre and uncleared at that. I thought that it would be alright to go ahead and, since last writing to you, I have already ploughed four acres and seeded them with Oats and Peas, for the Winter feed, with a cover crop of Orchard Grass and Red Clover. I have also blasted out the remaining stumps and levelled it all by hand. Where the logs were already burnt off, (about five acres), I have seeded down with Orchard Grass and Clover. All this I shall lose if I do not take up the land.

The milk business has now doubled and I deliver twice a day and am making on an average $55 per month, after paying for feed. I cannot keep three cows on just my fifteen acres alone and so should have to sell one and give up some of my milk customers. Of course, I could sell this place for a good price and start again from scratch somewhere further up-country on cheap, uncleared bush-land, but I am afraid that I am now too old and worn out to begin all over again. I have taken a lot out of myself, clearing this place. The Indian half-breeds around here call me "The Old Man by the Lake", so I suppose that I look it now. I certainly feel it and my hair and beard are quite grey and I am only twenty-seven this year.

I have discovered that I have two other families living near me now as neighbours. There is a pair of Peregrine Hawks, very handsome birds, who are nesting in the burnt-out crown of a very tall Douglas Fir. The tree must have been struck by lightning. Their nest is the size of a large wheelbarrow. It is incredible to watch the male bird flying back with his building material – quite large branches in his beak and talons. He is building far faster than I did!

The second family is a pair of Bald-headed Eagles. They are not actually bald but, from a distance, their snow-white heads give the impression of being completely unfeathered. I think they must have two chicks in the nest as I can hear two quite distinctly differing and furiously hungry cries. The Eagles are enormous, with a wingspan of about seven feet. Mac tells me that they can weigh anything from eight to sixteen lbs. or more and can live as long as fifty years. Their eyesight is incredible. From a mile up, you suddenly see one swooping down on some poor prey in the bush or, with one plunge of its beak, picking up an unfortunate Blueback Trout straight out of the river – a fish which can weigh as much as four lbs. at this time of the year. How strong these birds must be! My Eagles will outlive me and still be fishing here when I am long gone.

As McRae wanted his boat back, I have started to build my own boat, a canoe like the Indians' own. I have been watching them making theirs and thought I would have a shot at it. They build different types and sizes. On the coast, they have canoes for voyages, which can carry an enormous number of people. One has a length of about eighty feet with an eight ft. beam, but they also build much lighter ones for racing, to hold a crew of eleven men. Beautiful boats to watch, especially when they hold their races here on the lake.

Well, I am attempting to build a simple one for fishing, about seven feet in length. I have already felled a straight Red Cedar, which was growing very conveniently near the water's edge and have trimmed it and chosen the best section for the canoe. After removing the bark, (and storing it in my woodshed for the Winter fires), comes the most difficult and tedious job. It is to hollow out the log with chisel and maul and a light-weight axe. A fearfully slow, painstaking task because you must not make any mistake or you have ruined it all. I am also burning out part of the centre to make the chisel work easier. The outside has to be shaped with the same tools and also with an adze, which I borrowed from Mac. This is as far as I have got up to now, but I think that I have got the log into a good shape and thickness.

Next week, I will start on the really tricky part. You fill the hull with water and drop red-hot stones into it. In theory, as the wood expands and softens in the steaming water, you have to force the sides of the canoe apart with thwarts, (which, of course, you have cut and prepared in advance), in order to give the canoe the right width and curved lines. You then smooth the boat inside and out with a chisel and adze and fasten your cross-pieces to the inside of the gunwales. You should scorch the outside of the canoe to kill off any grubs that may be living in the wood, but I do not think that I am skilled enough to do this with-out maybe burning the boat, so I must just hope for the best.

Then, with a paddle and a wooden bailing-dish, your outfit is complete. You sit in the canoe cross-legged with your thighs pressed along the gunwale and with the foot on the paddle side in front and the other foot tucked away under you. A bit tricky to explain. Well, that is all the theory and I will report later just how it all turned out in the practice. It will still take days and days to complete.

Gerald and Faith are pretty fit. Claudia will start school in the Fall. Faith has taught her up to now but she feels that the child needs to spread her wings a bit and also have the chance to make friends. I will pay all the school fees. Claudia is an attractive seven-year-old, always happy and very intelligent. Faith is also teaching her the piano and she is making great strides. Did I tell you that Gerald bought the old "Steinweg" upright off George when "The Fens" was sold up? Claudia already plays the easier pieces from Mendelssohn's "Lieder ohne Worter" just beautifully, and she also draws everything she sees, from buckets to birds, just like her mother. For next Christmas, Gerald and I are clubbing together to give her a second-hand bicycle, so that she can ride to and from school, but only when she is a little older. Her first year, she will travel with two other children in a buggy. John is, of course, not yet old enough for school. He is only three years old next July.

Charles has left Vancouver and he and George are both living in Victoria. Someone saw them in the city, driving in a smart new motor-car and looking fit, fat and prosperous. George sold the new property for a large profit, so I hear. Did I tell you that he married again? Charles is doing very well in the car trade. He is separated from his wife. What a mistake that was! Our paths never cross now.

Tennis has become all the rage but I am far too stiff to play the game and anyway have none of the right togs or a racquet. Do you remember teaching Arthur and me on our court at home? What infinite patience you showed and what fun we had! I can still taste the cellar-cooled Lemon Barley drink which you always made for us thirsty boys!

My best love to you and I hope to hear from you again soon, as I am most anxious to settle the payment for my new land.

Ever Yr. loving Nephew,
William

P.S. Can you decipher this lengthy screed? My kindest regards to Miss Wheeler. What a charming photo that is of you both in your garden. Many thanks.

THE FIFTH YEAR

Skeecullus,
Duncans Station.   10th Dec., 1913

My dear Aunt,

This is to wish you and Miss Wheeler a very happy Christmas and a healthy and prosperous New Year. I am sorry not to have written sooner. Sometime last August, I received a very snorty, official letter from the family lawyer. I had not realised that Father had tied all the capital up so that I can only receive the annual interest and cannot touch the spondulicks, "because of your lack of responsibility where all financial matters are concerned". Charmingly worded and right to the point. Well, I was hoping for too much, as usual.

So I have paid the former owners another lump sum out of my savings and made an arrangement to pay them off as best as I can. I had done too much work to let this land go.

I had good crops this year, including about twenty tons of hay. It should see me through the Winter. I now have four cows, all nearly pure-bred Jerseys. They have paid for themselves more than twice over and are doing well. I was lucky to get a young Jersey bull at a Sale for only $60. His owner had once refused $350 for him when he was eight months old, from a Government farm. He is pure-bred and registered as "Lakes Model Lad" – such a suitable name for a bull living here. His father, (an imported prize-winner), cost $3,600 and his mother $3,000, so he is likely to be worth a lot of money one day. He is now sixteen months old. His former owner left the country suddenly and needed instant cash, which I, for once, had!

My brood sow had her first litter about ten weeks ago.

Nine in number. I have kept the best two sows and sold the rest for $4 each. My sow, "Belinda" is a Yorkshire and I gave $4 for her about a year ago. My boar, "Bertram", was a present from a friend last Christmas. He is a pure-bred registered Berkshire.

My milk round now clears me on an average over $60 a month all year round, after paying for feed. My young horse is growing. He weighs about 1,200 lbs. already and I am gradually teaching him, (*not* breaking him in, as I do not believe in that treatment). I got some strong, second-hand harness in the Saturday Sale at Duncans last week and hope to be able to afford a second-hand gig soon. I gave $12 for the harness. It is worth at least $35.

I now have twelve acres under plough, three acres of hillside pasture cleared, seven acres logged and seeded, (a good pasture), and another eight acres off which I am cutting cordwood, (which is firewood for cooking and for heating my stove). That should last me for five years at least.

There was some good Grouse shooting on a friend's place this Fall but the birds seem to move far quicker than over the Yorkshire Moors. Or are my reactions now so much slower?

I have two excellent wells with beautiful water, one twelve feet deep, which supplies the shack, and the other one twenty feet deep for the stock. The water comes to the shack by gravitation so there is no pumping needed. I did enough of that at "The Fens" to last me a lifetime!

Four years ago, my place was only all standing timber and bush, so thick that even a dog could not get through it. I hope that I have not tired you with all this rigmarole about myself and my doings but it is my whole life. Sometimes I get very lonely indeed and pretty heart-sick

THE FIFTH YEAR

and long to see the Old Country once again. They tell me that times are changing over in Europe and that life there is not what it once was. I do realise now that I did not properly appreciate my wonderful home life, and all the comforts, pleasures and security when I had it.

I shall drink to you both on Christmas Day, which I will spend as is our custom over at Gerald's place with his family, after going to Church with them and putting a wreath of evergreens on Antonia's grave. That is our yearly ritual. Claudia makes the wreath quite alone.

Please give my best love and all good wishes to any-body who may still remember me. So sad that old Sykes died shortly after you left the family home, but it was a good age to go. I am delighted to hear how happy you are in your new home in the mountains. I never thanked you properly for taking dear old Sheppy with you to Scawfell, to enjoy his last year on those beautiful fells. It is good to know that you buried him near you, in the garden.

Much love to you, dear Aunt, and my best wishes to Miss Wheeler.

Ever Yr. affec. and also very stupid Nephew,
William

THE SIXTH YEAR
1914

Skeecullus,
Duncans Station.   15th August, 1914

My dear Aunt Bella,

This is just to tell you that I have sold up everything out here and that I am sailing over to the mainland the day after tomorrow to enlist in the Canadian Expeditionary Force.

Even after settling all my many debts, I have still managed to leave Faith with quite a tidy sum to help with Claudia's education, for she is a clever child. I have also made my Will in Claudia's favour and written to our family lawyer to inform him, with a copy. The price of land had soared again and also my stock was worth quite a pretty penny. I have not been altogether a failure out here.

We have never heard a single word from Carlo since he returned to Italy, over three years ago now. I do well understand his silence, but for both his and for Antonia's sake I feel responsible for Claudia's future. I am very fond of my small niece and she of me, I think. Life out here is very tough for Gerald and Faith and it will be a great struggle for them to bring up and educate their little boy, without having also the burden of Claudia's education, clothing, etc.

Of course I will have to enlist under a false name, because of what I did all those years ago and so, should anything happen to me, I will give Faith's name and address as my next-of-kin. She promises to inform you should anything happen, but of course I will write to you from France. Maybe I can pay you a short visit while on the way?

I really did try so very hard but I just could not make it here alone. I never found any man willing to share my existence with me. All my life, I have never been able to judge the difference between my capabilities and my ambitions. Now I see that I have always grossly over-rated the former and that my fool's paradise is only a draughty shack on mortgaged land.

Looking back, I think that the great mistake was that I did not serve that prison sentence and then come out here, steerage, with nothing but my youth and my strength, to wander slowly westwards, feeling and working my own way, like hundreds before me. The way that Father did. Mother organised everything for me, as she had done my whole life. I was to travel out like a gentleman, with a gentleman's luggage and a generous remittance from home. At all costs her standards had to be maintained. My life has been so fashioned by her and bound up with hers that almost nothing was left of the individual me. Even my athletic sports were performances to please her and make her proud of me.

Antonia, I now realise, had come out under quite different circumstances. I had been thrown overboard – but into a lifeboat, fully equipped. She just jumped into icy water. She had such strength of character and, possessing such versatile abilities, she was able to turn her hand to just anything and make an instant success of it. She was determined to make good out here and she saw not a single difficulty that could not be overcome, eventually. From the moment that I arrived, I felt that she was absolutely appalled at what a slow, untalented, spoiled and lazy fellow she had for a younger brother. She was patience itself with me, in those first weeks, and gave me more good advice, support and self-confidence than I had had in the whole of my life. You know that it was only after Father's death that I learnt from him in his letter to me that she was only my half-sister? Perhaps that enabled her to see me so clearly and to love me for what I am, with all my weaknesses and failings. She understood me, through and through, and I will never forget that first evening at "The Fens", while I was unpacking and she sat curled up on my bed, that she said to me, "You are not wicked, William for only the strong can be wicked and you are so weak, so lost." That gave me the courage to start again.

When I was sent out here, my whole established world fell into pieces and, after darling Antonia's death, in my overwhelming desire to prove myself to you all, I rushed at life and made many rash and over-hasty decisions. I seem to have handled everything badly. She could have helped me so much but she only had the time to show me the way, leaving me at the signpost.

My fate has led me to this particular patch of earth, and here I have found myself. I know now who I am. I know now how to use my time, not just to waste time, to fill in time but to *live* time. There were so many questions which I have asked myself, especially in the snowed-in Winter months, sitting alone by my fire, smoking my pipe. I asked many questions and I found the answer, because there is only one answer to all the questions that one asks – just discover yourself, find out who you are.

The day that the War was declared against Germany, I suddenly knew who I was and felt absolutely certain that I do not belong out here. Now, for the first time, I understand the men who packed up and left here to go to fight in the Boer War. For them, that war was an honourable escape from untenable situations, as this war is for me. England has offered me my chance. Evening after evening, I have sat here alone on the steps to my shack, just watching the slow setting of the mid-Summer sun across the lake, putting my thoughts in order.

I am deliberately joining-up because that gives me my only chance to return to my Homeland, to see my own countryside, breathe the air, hear the English song-birds, see the familiar landmarks just once more and also to pay my respects at the Parents' graves. Perhaps to get a glimpse of you and Scawfell again?

Then it will be out to France, to do my bit, just one anonymous soldier among thousands. I hope to be able to join the Medical Corps, as I am not really a fighting sort of a chap, but I am very strong and heavily built and might be able to help other men. Perhaps I can serve my King and my Country better than I served my family. I promise you that I will try my very best to be an honest soldier.

Well, that's that, isn't it?

God bless you, my dear Aunt.

Ever Yr. loving and most grateful Nephew,

William

P.S. In your last letter, you enquired about my canoe. It sank.

THIS WAS THE LAST letter but at the bottom of the deed-box lay a plain envelope. It contained a medal and a short note, written by Aunt on May 17th, 1920:—

"This is the Distinguished Service Medal which was awarded to your Uncle William Newton-Lanes posthumously, for extreme bravery. He had enlisted, under the false name of William Lee, as a Private in the Canadian Army Medical Corps and he landed at Plymouth on October 16th, 1914, with the first 33,000 men of the 1st. Canadian Contingent. They completed their training in England and then crossed the Channel, landing in France in 1915 and proceeded to Flanders, to the very heart of the War.

He died of wounds which he received whilst rescuing his Officer and another Medical Orderly, who had both been severely wounded in an attack. He had carried them both to safety.

Your uncle William is buried somewhere in Flanders' soil.

Carlo Ghirlandi was killed, fighting some-where in northern Italy with the Italian Army against the Austrian Imperial Army in 1916. His grave is in Italy."

I just sat, for a very long time, holding the tarnished medal and the note in my hands, trying to bridge over all those years. There was also a large, discoloured envelope, which was stuck fast with mildew on the bottom of the box. I had to prise it off gradually with a blunt knife.

THE SIXTH YEAR

This envelope contained two copies of a photo, taken on the front porch of this house, sometime in Summer. Uncle Gerald and Aunt Faith, (she is very pregnant), are standing, arm-in-arm, on the top step, the proud house-owners. Uncle William is leaning decoratively against the porch, a Wisteria shoot in his long fingers, looking slim, elegant and very amused. I remember that sardonic look of his!

Sitting on the third step down is a little girl in a light muslin frock with a broad ribbon around the waist. She is wearing dark boots and her long, straight, black hair is held back in an Alice-band.

Beside her, seated one step lower, is a third man, very tall. His long legs trail on down the steps. He is dressed in light, close-fitting trousers, a dark jacket, a large bow-tie and light boots. He is holding the little girl's left hand in both his hands. The shape of his features and his swarthy colouring are unmistakable. It is my Uncle Carlo, and my face is his face.

Now, at last, I have found the answer to all my questionings, why I was so very happy all those eight years in Florence and the explanation for all my present restlessness.

I have found the real "I".

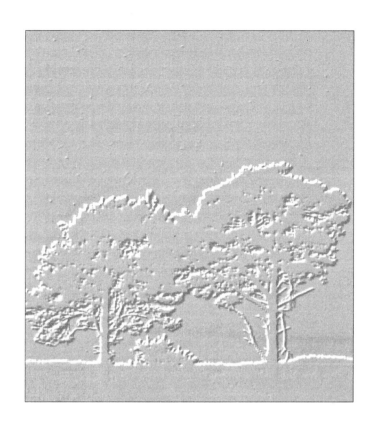

PART THREE

CLAUDIA'S STORY CONTINUED
– From Her Diary

SUNDAY, JUNE 4TH

I HAD JUST FINISHED reading all the letters when, around five o'clock, J knocked softly on my door and whispered, "I see that your light is on. Would you like to come out fishing with me before breakfast?"

We crept out to the car, with fishing tackle, baitbox and a thermos of tea and drove over to the marina where he moors his motorboat.

The iridescent and vermillion early-morning sky was simply breathtaking and there was not a soul anywhere about as we set off for the shallows around the point. J soon stopped the engine and we drifted in with the tide, right below the high, bare cliffs, where the cormorants and the Franklin's gulls nest, and we dropped our lines and fished in silence.

I caught a small rock cod pretty soon and then J got two beauties during the following half-hour, but that was all our luck and, as I had lost three hooks on dogfish, we decided to have a hot mug of tea with rum, before turning for home.

As I handed J his tea, I told him that I had planned to give him the answer to his marriage proposal on our way back from church this morning. But now something had happened that had completely altered my whole life. I told him how I had found the deed-box with the letters and the photo.

J was wonderful. Before saying anything, he poured us

both a second mug of tea and laced it very generously with the rum.

Then he said, "This must be a terrific shock for you but also what a marvellous discovery! Now you know that you've inherited your artistic gifts from both parents, as well as your obvious talent for languages, and so everything has summed up to make you what you are, a really international person and artist. Now surely, everything falls into place for you, doesn't it?" He grasped my hand and held it tightly. "There should be no more problems for you and now I, too, understand many things which were not clear to me, events which did not fit together. You know, when we were children, there were often sudden silences between Dad and Mother when we came into a room. Oh! you remember that, too?" I nodded.

"There's really only one big problem and that's Mother. Shouldn't you tell her that you've found this box? She must have known all along just whose child you really are, so that won't give her any awful shock. Only, maybe, make her feel just terribly guilty that you have found out, quite by chance, what I honestly think that she should have told you, years ago. I only wonder why she never did? It's not like Mother to conceal things or to play any sort of double game, is it? Well, we must just wait and see what she says. Would it help you if we told her together?"

After I had said that I wanted to leave everything in his careful hands and to his instinct, for she is, after all, his mother, he went on, "You know that I asked you out fishing as an excuse to get you alone and out of the house. This past week has been just Hell and I have so often wished that I could have done things better, but I just couldn't wait any longer. Ever since I saw you getting out of the plane, weeks ago, I knew that all my life I have actually only wanted to be with you. Isn't that crazy? A lifetime gone by, with a happy, a really happy marriage, good children and now the three grandchildren and then you come back – into what is left of it. What have we got ahead of us? Ten, fifteen years at the most and maybe you are in any case already tied up over there. What do I really know about you since you grew up and left home? Actually, nothing. And I have the feeling that you don't really want me to know anything about yourself, either. Whenever I've asked you about your life, you seem to avoid giving a direct answer. And I? I've just stayed here in the valley, made a living and got older, while you went off, as you had to, to make a totally different life for yourself."

And so dear J talked to me, explaining himself, encouraging me to talk openly at last about myself, calming me and giving me the feeling that there is solid ground under my feet again and that it is now our common ground, and that there could be a future here, together.

We returned to the wharf and drove home with the three rock cod in the boot of the car as evidence for Aunt of just any normal, early-morning fishing trip.

AFTER LUNCH, SITTING IN AUNT'S ROCKING-CHAIR IN THE BAY-WINDOW.

This has all been written to show John, one day. I never really knew just why I had to get down all my thoughts in this diary, everything that has gone on in my head from the moment that I got his cable, aeons ago. Now I know. My grandparents' letters, Mother's one letter and all Uncle William's letters were meant for me. This diary is only for John.

FROM HER DIARY

Breakfast was such a happy meal; Aunt got up to join us for the first time and admired our little haul of fish. She is feeling much better because the weather is definitely going to change. That we saw in the colours of the early-morning sky. And so we decided to drive to church and not to walk. How right we were! The rector prayed for an end to the drought and we had hardly added our heartfelt "Amens" when the heavens opened, just as Uncle William described the end of the drought in one of his letters.

We farmers needed this rain badly but I could only think of "The Storm King", "The Monarch" and "His Master's Voice" all standing outside the cellar door with the bicycles and all the other odds and ends, and of Leonard Woolf's autobiography and six cushions getting ruined in the hammock. But Jim, bless him! had rescued everything in time and covered the goods from the cellar with a tarpaulin.

J is now down in the cowshed, repairing a leaking roof, and Aunt is dreaming, after a very good lunch, her hands twitching just like Higgins' paws, when he is off on one of his dream hunts.

I have made a sketch of them both – rather good. A working basis for a portrait, later.

J and I have decided to talk to his mother this evening, after tea.

I have very cold feet about it all.

SUNDAY NIGHT, JUNE 4TH

There is so much for my diary, so much to note down before I forget all that she said. I must try to remember everything and that's why I am writing through the night, sitting up in bed.

After our Sunday afternoon tea and while we were all still sitting at the table, I suddenly took a deep breath and started off, very quickly, to tell her that during the last day's clearing-out, down in the basement, I had found a tin deed-box which contained a medal and packets of letters. Perhaps it was wrong of me, but I had read them all.

After this rather defiant start, I paused, partly to draw breath but mostly because I didn't know how to go on and I looked at J for support. Now I had done it! J was just going to help me out, when Aunt suddenly burst out laughing, clapping her hands, crying, "Hurray! hurray! hurray! So you have found them at last!"

We sat, simply stunned, while she went rattling on.

"Oh! darling heart, I felt so *awful*, just lying in bed, being so chicken-weak and helpless while you ploughed your way through the entire house, so gallantly, through room after room. I was hoping you'd come across them, and I began to think that I must have destroyed them by mistake, but, as you both well know, that would have been very unlike me. Now I needn't search through any more of those damned shoe-boxes of yours!

"I knew, in my heart of hearts, all along, that the letters were somewhere safe but I had completely forgotten just where I had put them. So I had tucked them away in one of the old suitcases in the basement? What a joke, for now we have a beautifully cleaned and sparkling house *and* the letters! I've had them on my conscience ever since that

FROM HER DIARY

215

beastly heart attack. The one thing I have been praying for is that you would come home, just as quickly as you could, and find them in time – I mean in *my* time, so that I could tell you all about them. Can you ever forgive me, Claudia?"

She laughed and laughed but suddenly the laughter turned to over-wrought tears of relief, so we both kissed her and I held her close in my arms until she had calmed down again. It had all been a great strain for her. She had kept everything to herself for years and years and now, at her great age, she was being asked to account for her actions.

"But why, darling," I asked her very softly and gently, "why did you never tell me before? Why have you kept this secret from me, all my life?"

There was a long pause and she wiped her eyes.

"I suddenly feel so cold," she said. "Please let's light a good fire in the living-room and all sit cosily there and then I will try to explain," and J went off to do as she asked.

Slowly I helped her over and into the living-room and pulled her Queen Anne chair close up to the fireplace and covered her legs with her warm plaid.

"What about a brandy?" said J. "Let's put sundown forward an hour or two. In any case it's invisible behind those huge thunderclouds. I think we're all in need of a purely medicinal drink." He put the bottle and the glasses on a small table and we all sat together by the fire, just enjoying the silence, being close together and watching the growing flames.

She had a sip or two of her brandy and, after a while, she said, "What was your reaction to the letters, Claudia?"

It was so clever of her to make me talk first and to give herself time.

So I told her just how shocked I had been to read of my grandfather's as well as of Mother's past but especially to read of Mother's death and of all she had had to keep silent about in her life. Also that I had only realized after reading the letters that Mother had had the makings of a really gifted artist but had been beaten by circumstances.

I said I thought that, like many women, then and now, she lacked the guts to go at life alone. Of course I know that it was terribly difficult for women in those days, at the turn of the century, but she had frittered away her beauty, her strength and her talents just to make a background for all of us. God! what a wicked waste! And Uncle William had known that and yet he wasted his own life, too. I cried with rage and not with pity over his letters. He had such charm and humour, but was so weak. He never learned that life owes none of us a living. He still clung to that wealthy home, an eternal cadger.

I was in danger of letting my feelings run away with me, so I pulled myself together. I told Aunt that once I had started reading the letters, I wanted to find out all I could about the relationship between Mother and Carlo. It was clear to me that, unlike Moses, I was not simply discovered in the bulrushes but quite obviously conceived there on the shore, in their shelter, and that I was born, not with a silver spoon in my mouth but with a paintbrush in my hand — a classic example of prenatal influence.

Aunt loved that. We all laughed and sipped our brandies. The atmosphere was calm again. The fire had also caught very well and we were beautifully warm.

Then Aunt settled herself back in her chair and started to talk to us, very quietly and seriously.

"You have read all the letters and now you know the

truth and I do realize that, for you, the most important part of the whole correspondence is what you have discovered about your parentage. It was fate. It was all so strange and yet so predestined that I should be the one to get possession of those letters."

I asked her how that had come about.

"When war was declared in August 1914, William immediately decided to join up. We told him that he must put all his affairs in order. He asked me if I would like to have Antonia's little bureau and also her rocking chair as farewell presents. He also wanted Gerald, of whom he was very fond, to have two pictures – William's favourites. You know which ones they are, don't you? The water-colour of your old home, "The Fens", which your mother painted and which now hangs in my bedroom and your father's oil painting of the view across Lake Somenos, which has ever since hung over his mantelpiece."

We all three looked up at it, remembering.

"William sold his property to his neighbour. Then he sold all his stock and farm implements at the market and his bits of furniture and settled up all his debts. The day before he left for the mainland, Gerald and I drove over in the cart to fetch him back here, so that he could spend his last day and night with all of us. I see it all as clearly as if it were yesterday. We found him sitting in the sun on the steps of his shack, with his back against the padlocked door. The bureau and the rocking-chair and the two pictures were beside him. He had just finished sweeping out his place for the last time and so we brought everything over here, including the broom. Funny how one remembers details like that! We had given him an old suitcase for his things, as he had given your father all his cases and hampers when Carlo returned to Italy.

"William was laughing and joking and so full of fun, happier than we had seen him in years. I have never met anyone who could make one laugh as much as William did. He was a born clown and a marvellous raconteur. Do you remember how we all gathered round the piano after supper and sang the old songs and how, next morning early, we all drove down to Duncans to see him off at the station? Yes, I thought you would. I will never forget that day. And on the platform, he gave his dog over to John's care. Yes, Rufus. He lived another nine years, the old scoundrel. What a comic pair of hunting dogs he and your Goldie were!

"I am sure William knew that he would never come back here again. I even think that he wanted to die. How shall we ever know what really went on in his poor lonely head, all those years? The only two people whom he had ever really loved and trused in his whole life were gone – his sister and your father."

She stopped. She did not want to go on and we just sat and waited. John poked the fire to cover our emotion.

"Gerald put the bureau in the outhouse, because it had got so damp in William's awful little shack and the French polish was completely damaged and the drawers stuck and the lid was warped. Gerald was so busy with the harvest and one thing and another, that he didn't get around to repairing it until the winter, when he brought it indoors to work on in the evenings, by the warmth of the kitchen fire. Only then did he discover a secret drawer and there were all the letters."

"I wonder why Uncle William didn't keep Aunt Bella's letters, along with all the others," I said.

FROM HER DIARY

219

"I don't know, dear, but the secret drawer isn't very big. Anyway, we wrote to William, to the army address that he had left with us, telling him that we had found them and were keeping them here for him but we never heard from him after the one and only letter, telling us that he had landed safely in France."

We waited.

"Then I received the official report of his death, because he had named me as his next-of-kin and later came a little packet for me, containing his medal for bravery. Much later came a letter from his family's lawyer in Liverpool, saying that William had left everything in his will to you, Claudia. But that part of the tale you know already because it was his money that helped with your education and clothing and which got you over to London to study at the Slade School and start you off on your career. He did that for Antonia and for Carlo, that I know, darling, because he told me all his plans. After Carlo had left, I was his only outlet."

She was very moved and found it hard to go on. I looked at J but he gave me a tiny signal to stay still.

"All the other letters, William's written to his mother and to his Aunt Bella, were sent to me after Aunt Bella's death by her friend, Miss Wheeler. Aunt Bella had always kept in touch with us and Miss Wheeler felt that the letters should come to me and asked me to keep them for you. I read them all, then, and decided to arrange them in the right chronological order, which was probably the only time in my life that I have ever been methodical, and I put them away safely for you in that deed-box. How that box ever landed up in the basement, I really can't imagine."

She was irritated with herself for not being able to

remember but then, thinking very hard, she told us that after the two extra rooms had been built onto the house for John and Janet after their marriage, Uncle Gerald must have moved all the junk out of the bicycle shed and into the new dry basement.

"Yes, that is what must have happened. Now, why did I not tell you about your parents? Long before you left us to go over to London to study, I had decided that I could not tell you then. Your uncle and I had had time to do a lot of hard thinking."

She leaned forward and stroked my cheek very gently, smiling, and for a moment I had the feeling that she thought I was my mother. She had never looked at me like that before.

"You see, Claudia, all the people in your mother's family were torn people, not really knowing where they belonged or else living white-washed lives, secretive and silent, locking up cupboards full of family skeletons – your grandfather, grandmother, Antonia, William and even, when I come to look back at it all, even Aunt Bella, because I guess that her skeleton was her relationship with dear old Miss Wheeler. Don't look so surprised! I may be old but I know all about such attachments. They're nothing new. Think of the ancient Greeks, the island of Lesbos! That is why she understood William so well.

"In those early years, many people who came out to the various colonies of the old Empire had something to hide. In any case, everyone who emigrated was a sort of graft and, if they take, then grafts add to the beauty of the original plant but if not, they just die off. Most of us managed it, in those pioneer times, but some, like William, did not."

FROM HER DIARY

She stopped again. She was losing the thread. J sat dead still, but I felt that he was willing her to go on.

"Now your grandfather's life was quite different. His story was of a totally successful escape and a new start — and then he went back, to be caught in precisely the same snare again. The tragedy for him was that there could be no second chance. He had tackled his emigration magnificently, learning the language, the customs and the type of life on the land which was offering so much success to men like him. His whole heart was out there, in the Argentine, on the River Plate, where he built up such a fine new life. He must have simply worshipped Antonia's mother, who was probably not only very clever but also a most lovely and passionate young girl, and adored that very tall, fair Englishman, with his soft, beautiful voice and gracious manners.

"Antonia often described the life out there to me and I had a clear picture of the huge ranch, of the whole property, the landscape and of their social life. He had brought Antonia up to be completely fearless, like her mother. She broke in his horses better than any gaucho and, although only a child, she ran her father and his household perfectly. They were just everything to each other and then — well, you know what happened. He threw it all away, to live the rest of his life trapped by that paragon of virtue, that cold marble pillar of the English establishment — with that second wife, Antonia's step-mother.

"There was, of course, no question of Antonia returning home alone to the ranch, as her father had had to sell up everything out there in order to re-start his life in England. He never got over what he had done, both to himself but, even more, to her. However, because he was a very clever man, he protected himself behind a magnificent facade of social and financial success. Antonia knew, and he knew that he had not fooled her and so, in the end, she could bear it no longer and she left him to go his way and she went hers, but her thoughts were often back on the ranch on the River Plate."

I asked Aunt about Arthur, for she had gone off into a dream, gazing, unseeingly, into the fire.

"Arthur? Now Arthur was the only one in that family with his feet firmly on the ground. He had studied hard and worked hard with only one aim – to get away from that home and that mother as quickly as possible and to make his own life and have his own family. He got as far away from "Oakleigh" as he could, first up in Scotland and then later down in London. His wife, Olivia, had wonderful parents and sisters. Her family home was filled with affection and laughter and many interests, as her father was a journalist and her mother an artist, but it was an impoverished home and regarded by the Newton-Lanes as impossible for a son of theirs to marry into. But Arthur and Olivia together made the best of both their worlds. It was a life-long partnership that survived all the ups and downs and Olivia's ill health triumphantly.

"Aunt Bella? She had no money of her own, except a little pin-money, and she was just an unpaid home help for your grandmother. Aunt Bella hated "Oakleigh" and sold it just as soon as she could, after inheriting it in your grandparents' wills. And then she too moved as far away as possible, up to the Lake District, with Miss Wheeler, and built a new future for herself, at last. Luckily she inherited in time! And William backed her up over that. And Arthur. He was a fine, generous man and fond of her.

FROM HER DIARY
_____

"And now we come to poor, darling William. William, the elder son of that rich, domineering, selfish mother, had never been the sort of ambitious son for whom she had hoped, never fitting into her pattern, although he did try, desperately, to be a good athlete. There, at least, he succeeded in pleasing both his parents, but all the time that boy was simply searching for warmth and affection from anyone, anywhere. And that is how he came to get into very dubious company and to be blackmailed. He stole from the bank where he worked, meaning to put the money back, but there was an unexpected auditors' check-up and he was found out. Dear William, he always did everything the wrong way around. He was very foolish and very weak, but not really a wastrel nor wicked.

"When he came out here, I did my best to explain his character to Carlo because, when he first saw William, he was furious that this spoilt, finely dressed dandy of a young brother was only going to be yet another burden on poor Antonia's back. I'm glad that I could do that and eventually, after her death, bring them together before Carlo went back to Italy. For William was a dear, kind, generous and loving fellow at heart and so amusing, turning every misadventure into a riotously funny story. And so, with his mother's death, he finally escaped. How very wicked some mothers can be!"

That remark, coming from her, whom I had never in my life heard censuring anyone, surprised me so much that I must have shifted in my chair.

"And now to you, darling. You asked me why I did not tell you about your parentage. It is very simple. I just could not bear the thought of burdening you in any way with all this past. You had to grow up a free child. Gerald and I were both so delighted when you first started to show signs that you had inherited your parents' gifts and when, as a child, you said that you were determined to become an artist, we knew that this was definitely going to be your direction in life. Of course we wanted you to have the chance to go to Europe to study with really good teachers and to develop yourself. William wanted that too, more than anything else, and his death made that possible. We ourselves could never have afforded to do that for you. I only wanted you to grow up here and to leave this house which has always been your home, thinking of yourself as a Canadian, born out here and belonging here, your roots in this valley – not grafted on but an indigenous plant, like the dogwood, which we both love so much, darling."

She smiled, that same smile and stroked my cheek again.

"Perhaps we should have told you when you were quite small but then your mother's husband, George, was still alive and living in Victoria with your half-brother, Charles, and we did not want any unnecessary gossip – things do have a way of getting out. Then, when George and his second wife were both killed in that car accident, it was somehow too late, for you were already far away in Europe. Was I not right? I did not want to unsettle you with the true story, with an Italian father and an Argentine grandmother of Spanish descent. You have become international through your art but deep down inside yourself, you must surely feel that you have got all your strength from this earth here, and that that is what has preserved you as you are, still unspoilt and trusting, perhaps rather ingenuous but very, very tough. Maybe all this sounds to you like the ramblings of a silly old woman, which indeed I am, but

I know that was the only way, all those years ago, that I could send you out into a very difficult world from the shelter of this protected valley. Now do you understand and can you forgive me?"

We kissed each other, and then we sat, all three of us holding hands, watching the burning logs shift and send fireworks of sparkling flames up the deep, stone chimney.

"Now I am feeling very, very tired, dears, and I think that I must get back to my bed. Tomorrow I will tell you all that I can remember about my darling Antonia and Carlo."

As we were helping her back to her bedroom and as J was just going over to the window to close her curtains, she called him back. The rain was beating down outside.

Gazing into the dripping darkness, she murmured, almost to herself, "Carlo, dear Carlo. It was a night just like this, Antonia said. He had been searching for a job, any sort of work, travelling all day from farm to farm with no luck and he was really in despair. Then, suddenly, he saw lights burning in a distant home across the lake. It was "The Fens". He thought that he might as well try his luck, just once more, or at any rate ask if he could sleep overnight in the barn. He struggled on for another mile through the bush and then over the muddy marshland. Only Antonia heard the knocking at the kitchen door. She went to open it and there stood this young Italian, in the drenching rain, so soaked and cold that he could scarcely speak. And that very evening, it all started. And he — he stayed on, to be near her. Oh! how they adored each other! Now I really am so tired but so very happy that I have been able to share the burden of these secrets with both of you.

"Goodnight, my darlings, and I will tell you both all the rest of the story tomorrow."

Monday, June 5th

But she never did, because she died in the night, quite peacefully in her sleep, while I was sitting up in bed, writing for hours and hours, putting down all that she had told us, in her own words, while they were still fresh in my memory.

Sunday, June 11th

We buried Aunt yesterday, in brilliant sunshine, John and I and his girls, who flew down from Kamloops and Prince Rupert with their husbands. Hundreds of people from the length and breadth of our valley came too, all our people, all our folk of so many different backgrounds, European, Indian, Chinese, Pakistanis, all came to remember a friend or to revere a grand old lady. People said that there had not been a funeral like that for decades.

After everyone had gone, John drove me across the valley and over to Mount Skeecullus. The present dirt road ends about where Uncle William must have tethered his horse, all those years ago. It is still a long and stiff climb up the mountainside. On the trail, we passed an Indian lad, crouched by a large boulder, staring with blank eyes across the valley towards the setting sun. John took a photo of me on the summit, looking out east across the Cowichan Valley and over to Georgia Strait. Tonight he developed it in his dark-room.

"I've made two copies. Keep one always with you, just to remember it all until you come back again."

FROM HER DIARY

LATER

Now I am going to start packing for I fly back to Vienna tomorrow. Not to stay, for I have talked everything over with J and decided to sell my studio and send my personal possessions – pictures, books, music, treasures all over here. Then I will travel to Rome to see if I can find any trace of what happened to my father. Somewhere I may find a grave? Or perhaps a family? And then I will go to Florence, where he and I both studied, and spend a few quiet days there, a bridging-over time, to sort out myself and my future.

J says that he will wait for me here, in the home that Carlo, my father, designed and built with J's father's and Uncle William's help. I now know who I am. That is the answer to so many questions. My future years will be lived here with J. We are old enough to give each other plenty of leeway, but to find in each other the security and warm affection for which we have both been searching. And I can set up an easel anywhere. It is the inspiration that counts.

MONDAY, JUNE 12TH

In half an hour, J drives me to Pat Bay airport where I arrived only five weeks ago. My life has changed completely, and I can only thank my family who left me an inheritance that has made my life so uniquely rich.

Putting on my hat for the journey, I have just looked at myself in the mirror – eyes, angles, intensity. The first portrait when I return will be a self-portrait, for as much as this diary has really been a self-analysis, so a self-portrait will be a statement on canvas of what it has taken me my whole life to discover – the person behind my face.

CLAUDIA'S STORY CONTINUED

I am going to put this diary on John's desk, before I leave. In this short span of time, he and I have both learned to speak to each other, hiding nothing, and to listen better than we have ever done before. There will be no silences between us.

AFTERWORD

THE CENTRAL THEME of this story is the discovery of some letters, written between 1909 and 1914, by an emigrant son to his mother, living in England.

Years ago, I had decided to sail out to Canada, thinking that I might live there, only to discover just before the Polish ship, *Stefan Batory*, left Rotterdam Harbour that, although British-born, I could only stay in Canada for a maximum of six months. I must then return to Europe and apply for immigration status at the Canadian consulate in Vienna, where I had been living for the past 16 years.

Having burnt my boats, I decided to make the very best of that half-year, enjoy the voyage and then discover something of this vast country, Canada. So I rapidly exchanged my single ticket for a return.

From Montreal I drove for seven days in my small Fiat 500 car, with my bastard sheepdog, through very wintry April weather, landing up in Maple Bay, on Vancouver Island. Here I had an old and lonely relative, who had been writing me letters that were increasingly worrying. She had emigrated to the island about 40 years earlier and, being not only a delightful Irish eccentric but also very lazy, she had never bothered to finish unpacking. In a grime-covered trunk in her chaotic cellar, I found the letters.

The six months were up, and I returned to Vienna to start up a new life there. Years later, after retiring, I decided that the letters were really meant to be discovered by me and that I must somehow make these relics from a long-bygone period in the history of Vancouver Island available.

And so I wrote this tale, leaving the reader to guess what is real and how much is fiction.

ELIZABETH LATHAM